– Liverpool –
MMXXV

MOTIVES
UNKNOWN

dead ink

First published in Great Britain in 2025 by Dead Ink,
an imprint of Cinder House Publishing Limited.

Print ISBN 978-1-915368-91-1
ePub ISBN 978-1-915368-92-8
Kindle ISBN 978-1-915368-93-5

Cover design by Alex Robbins / alexrobbins.co.uk
Typeset by Steve J Shaw / white-space.uk

Printed and bound in Great Britain by Clays Ltd, Elcograf S.p.A.

www.deadinkbooks.com

 Supported using public funding by  **ARTS COUNCIL ENGLAND**

Funded by UK Government

 MIX
Paper | Supporting
responsible forestry
FSC® C018072

MOTIVES UNKNOWN

NEW NORTHERN CRIME

Edited by Nathan Connolly
& Harriet Hirshman

dead ink

INTRODUCTION

What connects the hardboiled nihilism of James Ellroy's *The Black Dahlia* to the comforting cosy antics of Richard Osman's *The Thursday Murder Club*? How can the open-ended social critique of something like Don Carpenter's *Hard Rain Falling* or Elizabeth Hand's *Generation Loss* be found on the same shelf as the closed-room mysteries of George Simenon's Inspector Malgret series or Agatha Christie's Hercule Poirot books?

For most literary genres there is a sensible collection of identifiers that mark books out as belonging together, but for crime there seems only one – the presence of a crime! The genre is therefore pinned together by what is essentially a mechanical plot point macguffin around which everything else revolves. Therefore, perusing through the crime shelves of your local bookshop is likely to be somewhat overwhelming as names like Anthony Horowitz, Sir Arthur Conan Doyle, Susie Dent, Derek Raymond, Ann Cleeves, Dashiel Hammet, Chester Himes, James Patterson, Gillian Flynn, Rob Rinder, Raymond Chandler, Patricia Highsmith, Lee Child, Val McDermid, S. A. Crosby, and Cornell Woolrich all jostle for your attention.

This is to say nothing of the crime genre in translation where, amongst others, Japanese, Italian, French, Swedish and

Korean authors bring their own cultural interpretation of the genre and their country's social mores. Leonardo Sciascia's subtle and vague tales of Sicilian political corruption may share some surface level thematic similarities with Stieg Larsson's *Millienium* trilogy, but that is where the similarities end and the two couldn't be further apart. The examination of corruption might pair them together, but Sciascia is more interested in the pervasive social decay that it brings about whilst Larsson delves into the psychological repercussions of sexual violence and exploitation to examine the corruption and excess of the capitalist class.

This, I think, highlights the crime genre's greatest strength. No matter where a crime book is from, or where it falls on the airport bookshop paperback to revered clothbound literary classic scale, the true power of the genre is in that mechanical plot point macguffin that sets everything in motion. The gunshot that, like a starting pistol, enacts the murder and sets off the investigation or the escape or the revenge is ultimately nothing more than the starting action of the Rube Goldberg machine that keeps you pinned to your seat and turning the pages. To understand what the genre is about requires us to zoom out to look at the whole – the crime at the heart of a crime story is a narrative tool for transgressing against the normal ways of society so that we may more clearly see the critique of the *real* problem.

In Ellroy's *The Black Dahlia* it isn't ultimately all that relevant who actually killed Betty Short, because throughout the investigation we become witness to all the corruption, degeneracy, and exploitation of late-1940s California that set the stage for it to happen. Ellroy's trademark nihilism, then, is less of an affectation and more of a condemnation – particularly as the novel's conclusion takes place under the birth of the new Hollywood as the old Hollywoodland is torn down. The crimes against both the living and the dead Betty Short are the original sin that hangs over the Hollywood of today.

I've chosen to look directly at Ellroy here because he was a direct influence on the North of England's very own David Peace and his *Red Riding Quartet*. Peace takes Ellroy's staccato typewriter writing style and adopts it wholesale along with his nihilism and his lens of the sweeping historical epic, but brings it to Yorkshire and eventually Lancashire and Merseyside. Peace also brings in the very Yorkshire influence of the Brontës and their gothic sensibilities. Only he takes this gothic sensibility and turns the dial up to show that the mid-1800s has nothing on the 1970s when it comes to decay and degradation. The trick is almost absurd, but it cleverly draws the reader's eye to his thesis of societal rot and systemic corruption.

It is similar in style to another northern crime writer, Manchester's Ted Lewis. Although Lewis eventually moved to London to make a living as a writer, it is telling that he brings his titular character home to the North in *Jack's Return Home*, or *Get Carter* as it would later be known. Lewis was one of the instigators of British Noir and his gritty hardboiled works about enforcers, convicts and pornographers dabble with the same gothic undertones as Peace to examine the deterioration of the urban social contract.

Ultimately the crime genre thrives because of its versatility. It is capable of being endlessly reinterpreted, reappropriated, and reinvented. Crime is, after all, universal. Inspired by the work of David Peace and Ted Lewis, as well as Benjamin Myers and LJ Ross, we wanted to start a new list at Dead Ink focused solely on crime fiction from the North of England. The versatility of crime combined with the dramatic and atmospheric locales of our home felt like a natural combination for good storytelling.

But we hit a hurdle.

After two years of speaking to the good, the bad, and the ugly of London's literary agencies we had nothing. Despite a long and illustrious tradition of crime from the North of England it seemed that nobody was doing the legwork to find contemporary writers in the genre. It fell to us, then, and this book is the result of an entirely open call to unrepresented writers in the North or with a northern background.

Although what I originally had in mind was something hardboiled, gothic and seedy, as that's where I tend to enjoy most of my crime fiction kicks, the book that resulted from our call out is more varied than I could possibly have imagined at the start. It demonstrates that not only is crime writing in the North vibrant, but it is also flourishing across multiple styles and approaches.

Inés G. Labarta's 'What Has Sunk May Rise' is a somewhat cosy crime tale of the precarious nature of academic work inflected with references to Lovecraft. The story itself has a valid and serious point to make about desperation and the levels to which some would go to achieve professional security in the modern world, but it is also fun and seems to have a permanent sly grin that is hard not to be enamoured by.

Similarly, 'Table 4' by Abby Walker boils the crime drama down to the simplest of intrigues crossing work-life and domestic boundaries. A patron's overheard conversations lead our protagonist down a nail-biting spiral resembling a high-stakes thriller, but here it is matters of the heart and a sense of justice inherited from past failed relationships that push the narrative forward. It isn't murder, drugs, or espionage that provide the pace; all the hallmarks of the crime genre are present in what could be an anecdote you hear from a friend. It is in the telling that Walker transforms the domestic into the heart-racing.

We plunge deeper into the darkness in Dan Howarth's 'Off Book' as an actor commits himself to a role portraying a real-life killer. Though the story is serious and executed with aplomb there is something of Steve Pemberton and Reece Shearsmith's *Inside No. 9* about it – a bloody-minded perseverance to see a wild-eyed idea through to the end and witness in full its gratifying and inevitable conclusion. To do so requires a deep respect for the traditions and conventions of the genre, but it needs a wicked sense of humour too.

Conversely, 'What Gets Forgotten' by Joey McGarvey centres around the taboo subject of child killers, that is children that kill, and as such can never escape the horrifying cases of the recent past that traumatise the region. It is not a story with a sly grin, but neither is it callous or sensational. It adopts the point of view of one of the perpetrating children and asks the reader complex questions around judgement and culpability. It could be an approach deemed controversial, but McGarvey handles it with sensitivity and deftness.

Perhaps one of the most surprising finds in the book was Ewan A. Dougall's 'In Loving Memory' which manages to somehow fit an entire procedural into less than 6,000 words.

This alone would be an accomplishment worthy of applause, but what elevates it further is the difficult subject matter of historic guilt and failing memory. The story is complex and tightly composed, but still leaves room for flair in both the narrative and prose.

On a similar note of surprise is Lauren Archer's 'I Must Go Down' that is crime focused, but borrows much of its genre DNA from the weird and speculative branches of horror and sci-fi. In particular, the waterlogged Liverpool recalls horror legend Ramsey Campbell's *Creatures of the Pool* where denizens of Liverpool's past rise up through rain-soaked streets. The similarities are only surface deep, or perhaps subterranean would be more apt, but the unspecific and somewhat otherworldly setting of Archer's story demonstrates how far the crime genre can be pushed from its traditions and still remain a member of the family, illustrating how much of a playground it can be for talented writers.

The Merseyside connection continues with the brutal but benevolent 'Saving Kenny' by Stan Fenton. Inevitably because of the Liverpool setting and the bad-but-good anti-hero comparisons can be made to Scouse novelist Tony Schumacher's TV crime series *The Responder*. As a Liverpool-based publisher being able to draw upon such home-grown cross-medium comparisons is delightful, but also both stories are astute examples of how the crime genre can navigate complex moral questions around the rule of law and if it is possible to stay *good* when transgressing the boundaries of the state.

Taking a different approach, Dawn Nicholson's 'A Quiet Retribution' asks similar moral questions – this time along the well-trod path of vengeance and retribution. Only here, Nicholson uses a case of historic childhood sexual abuse as her example and, rather unusually, her protagonist is an elderly woman who refuses to let historic crimes go unpunished. I doubt anyone would sympathise a great deal with the villain of 'A Quiet Retribution', but it shouldn't go unnoticed how quietly transgressive the story is. Nicholson's choice of an elderly and unassuming woman as her agent of revenge goes against the established and normative expectations of the genre in order to highlight the justice system's historic failure to deliver meaningful resolution on cases as well as the role of communities in shielding and enabling perpetrators.

Beth Barker's 'Skeletons' is a nostalgic piece on the halcyon summer days growing up in a seaside town. It is imbued with an intimate sense of place and time, but also the claustrophobic intensity of youth. The writing is vivid, evocative, and born out of lived experience. In essence, it is writing that can't be faked.

Likewise, memory and nostalgia are evoked to different ends in 'The Crucible Summer' by Pete Hardy. Here, though, as we look back across decades tinged with regret and remorse, dark periods of the North's past are brought to mind such as the Yorkshire Ripper and the Moors Murders. The story grounds us in place and time and we are immersed in the culpability of the landscape and the history.

'Algorrhythmia' by David Lawrie is perhaps the most stridently *literary* story in the collection in that it is driven forward more by prose style and experimentation than narrative and plot, but it exists within a long tradition of prose envelope-pushing within the genre such as James Ellroy, David Peace, Dennis Johnson, and Jean-Patrick Manchette. Within this collection it displays that crime is not just a tradition composed of plot points, but can also be used to challenge boundaries of composition that opens up new possibilities.

There is also power in the crime genre to introduce and familiarise that which is alien to you, and different stories in the collection will be able to do that for different readers. For me, Andrew Hudson's 'The Ends' was the story that transported me to a place and situation I'd never before considered, let alone experienced – dealing drugs out of a minivan at a Young Farmers' Club. The-slice-of-life tale is imbued with small details and character quirks that make the unfamiliar real whilst being, at least for my lived experience, wholly original and novel. I think because of this unfamiliarity that I approached it with, it quickly became one of my favourites and brilliantly illustrates why we should look beyond our traditional boundaries for new talent. Frankly, we don't know what we're missing until we find it.

Putting together this book was not an exercise in finding enough talented writers, but whittling down all the talented writers enough that we could fit them in a book. I suppose that not every reader will be taken by every story, but that is sort of the joy of the genre – for each sub-genre of crime writing there is a reader, and what I think we have demonstrated in *Motives Unknown* is that the North of England has the talent not to be pigeonholed as a place for just one particular style. Northern writers are as varied and dazzling as the region itself.

Nathan Connolly

MOTIVES UNKNOWN

NEW NORTHERN CRIME

WHAT HAS SUNK MAY RISE
INÉS G. LABARTA

The Lovecraftian Manifesto for Surviving Academia

1. *Nobody can truly know how permanent posts are given, how articles in reputable journals are published or how projects get funded. What moves these threads behind the scenes cannot be comprehended by mere human minds.*
2. *Academia is a cult with arcane hierarchical levels, old-fashioned rules and blatant unfairness.*
3. *Lovecraft's 'What has risen may sink, and what has sunk may rise' predicts the crumbling of a system which doesn't work for the majority of us.*
4. *We must fight back against the dark forces controlling academia and, if needed, take Lovecraftian measures.*

We had reached our crisis point long before I urged us to take action. Lì was the one who said it out loud during our meeting: we can't keep going on like this. She was the smartest of us all, Lì. She had to be. The first Chinese PhD student to graduate into the English Literature department of our founded-in-the-Middle-Ages prestigious English university. Seventeen years later, she was still working as a teaching instructor, rolling temporary contract after temporary contract from October to

May. Raúl had only been in the same position for three years. Me, I was coming up to six. The three of us met at the Equality and Diversity committee in the department. Professor Johns had suggested it'd be a great CV item. When we got to the first meeting, we realised we were its only members (which was funny, considering how Lì and Raúl were immigrants, and I was gay, but I guess that's why Professor Johns and the others thought we were fit for the task).

After Lì had dared to put what we all felt into words, I started our Starving Postdocs Rebellion Group Chat. I said I was sick of getting so few hours of teaching during the academic year that I had to take a series of temporary jobs to survive. And I was sick of fighting for those hours like they were a golden prize. And if I ever asked for more, like an academic Oliver Twist, my head of department reminded me how lucky I was to be teaching at all.

'Do you even know how many other PhD students would be so glad to get even an hour of teaching experience?' she'd remind me. 'I had to beg everyone to keep you and the other postdocs in the rota, but I can't make magic with the budget numbers, you understand that, don't you?'

She knew I would do anything rather than go back to Lincolnshire, to my dad's farm in the bogs to milk cows to their death. I wasn't a farmer's daughter anymore, I was a scholar. Sure, my work was on Lovecraft, the twentieth-century horror writer who wrote *The Call of Cthulhu* and what many still considered trashy genre literature (in our department the big names were Shakespeare, Chaucer, Milton and the like, since we lived in a medieval town it seemed the research topics had also got stuck around that time period) but I still deserved a fairly paid, stable job in academia, damn it. Raúl nodded. He knew what I was talking about, having come all the way from Spain – that jobless Catholic shithole, as he called it – where he'd been beaten up by a gang of neo-Nazis for holding hands with another guy (who turned out to be his younger brother). Lì said she was tired of being invisible to the 'real' (that is, permanent) members of the department unless there was an extra load of marking because one professor or other had swanned off to a sabbatical. The union reps were useless, focused on the *Don't Cut Our Pensions!* fight. (Pensions? What pensions? Our temporary contracts didn't even include sick pay.) The professors were too busy writing shiny grant applications or being transferred to management; senior lecturers were swamped with admin since the university had decided to sack half of its admin staff; lecturers only took notice of us to offer us extra jobs like babysitting or working on their gardens, as if that would help our career prospects.

Lì, Raúl and I had all spent years completing our PhDs, sharing dirty student flats with rats and undergraduates, working weekends and holidays in pubs and shops to earn some cash, while spending nights reading journal articles so we could write the literature review for our theses. We had given up on having a social life, hobbies, spirituality, partners, children, a house. We were burnt out, broke, depressed. Isolated. Lì and Raúl lived countries away from their families, and I had severed all that linked me to Dad, the farm and his disapproval. In Dad's world, women didn't fancy other women, or leave their homes because they thought they were smarter than everyone else.

We'd all sacrificed way too many things to quit.

* * *

Of the three other postdocs in the department competing with us for the teaching hours, Lì said Sharon would be the easiest one to work on first. Sharon had short, bleached hair and wore chinos and oxford shoes. Her office was at the end of the corridor. Books, folders and student essays piled on the desk, the floor and the cheap, white shelves. Mouldy cups of tea she'd stolen from the staff kitchen and chocolate wrappers occupied any spare space. She hadn't bothered bringing personal items like family photos, posters from conferences she'd attended, trinkets from research trips. That she hated living in town wasn't a secret: from day one she would bitch about how much nicer Brighton was (she'd done her PhD there and, apparently, spent the best years of her life there, too). Brighton wasn't as windy, she said. Or as dark. Or as cold. And people were much friendlier, and they had modern art galleries, and exciting shows in the theatres, and a proper shopping centre. She couldn't wait to get out of here, so when we gave her the little push she was asking for, we were doing her a favour.

We began sending anonymous letters to her pigeonhole in the post room. That went on for weeks, but nothing happened. The parcel was my idea. I got inspired when I was dog-sitting for my research mentor. She had a gorgeous blue Great Dane she never had the time to walk. Lex. Shiny velvety skin, and long flappy legs, like a gangly teenager. That dog ate cans and cans of organic food (chicken and tomato with oregano and spirulina, better food than the baked beans I could afford) and shat small mountains I picked up with a plastic shopping bag. Those shit piles looked human. Or, in Lovecraftian terms, monstrous.

The day she got her special delivery, they told us that Sharon ran down the corridor shouting nonsense, stumbled inside our head of department's office and burst into tears. And that's how the legend about the parcel full of shit started going around uni. I know many still think it's all made-up. Who cares? A few weeks after that, Sharon was gone. She'd been accepted to another postdoc position in Bologna.

* * *

Dylan was next. We were still fine-tuning our tactics. With their immigration status, Li and Raúl couldn't afford a criminal record. Raúl, who had always been the sensitive one – his research was on dystopia in Kazuo Ishiguro's work – was also worried about the ethics of it all. (Ethics? I said to him. What ethics? Do you think that the universities who give us these shitty teaching contracts we can't live on have any ethics?) But, when Dylan arrived in the department, with a fancy postdoc scholarship, we all agreed he had to go. He was barely halfway through his twenties (he wrote his year of birth everywhere, including his social media bios) and had more confidence than he could manage. Thin blond hair brushing his shoulders, already balding on top of his head, which made the whole thing look sad. Black-rimmed glasses, mean grey eyes. He thought himself a renaissance man, destined to break all moulds. He also had OCD. Never stepped on white tiles when he walked around the department's corridors (only the black ones). I started noticing that right after he disclosed his condition to the Equality and Diversity committee; that is, to us.

Lì suggested we should paint all the black tiles white, at least on our floor, to give him a shock. But that was a crazy idea. Raúl volunteered to spy on him to gather some extra information. Raúl was a furry bear: six feet two, beard to his chest and a pair of old Doc Martens, full of holes, which he refused to get rid of. He was sweet and funny, the only staff member who the admin team regularly invited to their secret smoking spot in the parking space behind the department. That's where he heard all the gossip, and he started sharing bits with Dylan. Who could say no to a bit of department gossip? Raúl used his new friendship to infiltrate Dylan's office, which was how he noticed that all the books on the shelves were classified according to literary theories and, within those groups, alphabetically arranged.

We started changing the books' order when Dylan left for the night (I had an old key to his office, from the year it had been mine). He lived on the other side of town, the fancy side, away from the dirty student pubs and the homeless sleeping in doorways, so he had to take the bus and was unlikely to come back. Commuting was a delicate operation, he used to say: too early in the evening and the buses would be full of sweaty undergrads going home; too late and they'd be full of drunk undergrads going to party. It made me laugh, the way he said that, as if it'd been decades since he'd been a student. What a pretentious baby.

Dylan never reported his books changing places. We were subtle about it, only altering one, sometimes two titles at a time. His mood changed, though. He became irritable, looked over his shoulder more often and tried to stay in the office for longer. This dragged on for months until we came up with a more direct way of getting rid of him.

* * *

We waited for Dylan in the staff kitchen. It was Tuesday, seven in the evening, and his office light was still on. We sat on the old blue sofas, which were always stained with coffee and ink.

'Hey,' Lì said when Dylan came through the door. Raúl and I kept typing on our laptops as if we were too busy writing notes for our next academic article.

'You're working on thistle representations in the Bible and religious texts from the Elizabethan period, right?' Lì said. Dylan was one of those people who used every opportunity to talk about his research, so we were quite familiar with it.

'Yes, yes, that's why the department brought Julia Alexander in, so she could be my supervisor because she's an expert on botanical symbolism in the Bible, isn't she, and she's also the director of the International Association of Biblical Botanics and Metaphor.'

Lì nodded while pouring tea from her glass kettle into a chipped cup. She still looked like a twenty-something postgrad with a wrinkled shirt that was a bit too big on her, faded jeans and canvas shoes. Her silver mop of hair completely out of place. Even though she was senior to all of us postdocs, she didn't enjoy the respect that should have come with the position. We'd never formally discussed it, but we in our little group knew it was because of her research: the representation of period blood in Shakespeare's plays, a theme that almost every male academic I knew of had frowned upon, including Dylan. (I guess writing about periods in literature has always been controversial, but a complete PhD thesis? That's definitely pushing it.)

'You know? I was just thinking about Elia, you know Elia?' Lì said. 'Elia Hornberger? She's about to publish a monograph on the significance of the thistle in Biblical literature in the Elizabethan period too, and I think she also compares it to German literature as well, global research is in these days, right?'

'What? Who's this Hornberger?' Dylan said.

'A German scholar. I met her at a conference, a couple of years ago. I thought you may know her too. Your research topics are kind of similar, no? Anyways, her monograph is coming out soon... is it with Palgrave?'

'Bloomsbury,' I corrected Lì.

Elia Hornberger didn't exist until we made her up four months before. It had been a complex project: we created a fake ResearchNet profile for her that included the abstracts of six different articles she had published in very reputable journals. She also had social media (@DrThistle), and a website that we updated regularly. The profile image for both was the colourful cover of her upcoming Bloomsbury monograph with a rabid pink thistle flower on it (Raúl's photoshop skills came in handy there). We even wrote an article about the symbolism of the thistle in the book of Genesis and the letters of Katharina von Bora that was supposed to be part of the monograph, and which she had published on her website for free (researching for it, we all agreed, almost brought us back to those early years of the

PhD, when every task seemed an exciting adventure). All of this in the hopes Dylan would google her, which he did, right there in the staff kitchen with us. We all saw him going pale. He kept swirling a plastic teaspoon around his cheap instant coffee, spilling it all over the counter. He mumbled something, tidied up with a dirty tea towel that had been there for years, and poured what was left of his cup down the sink.

He didn't come back to his office the next day. Or the day after. The official announcement was that he'd had a mental breakdown and was taking leave. Lì, Raúl and I volunteered to teach Dylan's classes that term – earning some gold points with our head of department, who was desperate for cover. Our plan was working.

∗ ∗ ∗

Ned was next. He was a hard one. We liked Ned. He was chill, chatty. Always supportive, always available to go for a beer to vent. One of those postdocs who would knock on your door with an extra cup of coffee from the canteen. He kept a tally of everyone's birthday and organised cards and money collections beforehand. Which was a bit irritating, we thought. It didn't feel right giving money – the money we all struggled so much to keep in our bank accounts – to buy a ridiculously expensive fountain pen for a professor who made more in a year than we'd see in our entire lives.

'Ned's a bit too… joyful,' Raúl said. 'Don't you find that annoying? Must be the super-rich husband.'

'Ned is married?' Lì said.

'Yes, his husband works for Mastercard.'

'No way.'

'Lots of money, beautiful semi-detached house with a pool and a garden, a cute black pug...'

'No wonder he's always so happy,' I said. 'He doesn't even need this job.'

'I tell you what he doesn't need,' Raúl said. 'Scandal. One of the night porters told me he caught Ned making out with Paolo. In his office.'

'Who's Paolo?' I asked.

'An MA student. Tall. Curly hair. Pretty hot.'

* * *

It turned out Ned wasn't even that careful about Paolo. As if all that happened at the university stayed within the confines of campus. We snapped a few photos of them holding hands and cuddling in the beer garden next to the faculty. Ned's husband's email address was even easier to find with a fake LinkedIn profile.

The day after we sent the photos, Ned came to uni with puffy wet eyes, a heavy rucksack and his pug, Elliot, in a picnic basket. My office was next to his, so I came by to see if our plan had worked out.

'It's over,' he told me whilst I petted Elliot. 'He's kicked us out. He says he doesn't want the stinky dog because his cat, Maud, hates him.' Ned started crying. 'Can you believe that? He told me he loved dogs. And he kicked us out...'

I shook my head, letting Elliot drool all over my jumper.

'It'll be alright,' I said, although I hoped it wouldn't.

According to Raúl, Ned's husband was his main source of support. Losing that, the few hours of teaching Ned had in the department wouldn't be enough to get him through (he was clearly already used to having a comfortable lifestyle) and he'd have to look for a more reliable source of income. In other words, quit academia.

The day after, I went to my office at my usual time, six in the morning (I always loved it that way, silence, no emails, no first-year students shouting up and down the corridors). But as soon as I unlocked my door, I heard some barking. And then hushing. Had Ned spent all night in his office with Elliot? A couple of hours later, a sleepy Ned appeared in the staff kitchen: messy hair and morning breath. He was carrying a tote bag with a folded towel inside.

'I'm going to the gym before my seminar,' he said. It was obvious that the only thing he planned to do there was to take a shower.

* * *

We didn't tell anyone the first week. We knew that the longer Ned's situation went on, the worse it would be when everything came to light. To his credit, Ned had thought things through. He kept his food in the staff kitchen fridges (grapes, microwaveable dinners, milk, samosa packs and hummus). He showered at the gym and spent the night under his desk in a sleeping bag he shared with Elliot. We waited for two months. Then I went to the head of department to have a chat. She was a funny woman: hair dyed a blinding neon red and baggy dungarees from an extremely expensive brand that used things like plastic found in the ocean to make their clothes. Academics in higher positions like her thought their privilege gave them permission to be eccentric and edgy. But, if you ask me, they all looked like wrinkly teenagers. I said to her I was worried about the students. A few of them had complained their seminar tutor was acting strange. There were also some concerns amongst staff about this same tutor having his dog with him at all times. At this point, I sneezed. Dog allergies, I explained. And were there not some safety issues with having a dog in the department?

Ned was out that same week. No goodbyes, no explanation. And with him disappeared the dog barks at random times, the shiny black hairs on the white tiles in the corridors.

* * *

By then, we thought the chance that at least one of us would get a permanent contract was high. There were too many teaching hours that needed cover. I was so optimistic about this that I didn't take on the head of the department's offer – emailed to all PhD students and postdocs – of painting her writing hut for fifty quid next weekend. My days of doing random extra jobs to pay my rent were coming to an end. We had agreed that Lì should go first. She'd help us from above. At that point, though, things took an unexpected turn. The university decided they wanted fresh blood in the department.

* * *

Mike turned up at uni on a cold September morning. He was a medievalist expert on Viking and Nordic literature (which, in my mind, was the stuff Fascist and ultra-nationalist people raved about these days). Apart from the fact that he didn't have any neck – his rosy face simply narrowed to meet his chest and shoulders – he was cute. Always wore bright plaid shirts and light blue jeans with white trainers. Short corn-coloured hair.

During his first weeks, he proved to be extremely outgoing for a scholar. He didn't tiptoe around the department avoiding eye contact until people noticed him and introduced themselves. He went around all our offices and was very good at pretending to be interested in who we were and what we did. What bothered us the most was that he was a young, fresh thing, not much older than Raúl and myself, which made us all wonder how he had landed a permanent job so fast. What obscure deity had he prayed to so he could be granted such a miracle?

We invited him to drinks every Friday. Those first outings revealed that Mike had a brilliant CV. He had studied at a Russell Group university and taught in a few renowned institutions. He already had a monograph out with a prestigious publisher which was enjoying moderate success.

I was re-reading *The Call of Cthulhu* for the umpteenth time when I met Mike. Lovecraft's most famous story depicts the awakening of an ancient deity full of tentacles, Cthulhu, so terrifying that every human that so much as gazes at it is rendered insane. I had been wanting to write an article about interpreting this story through a Marxist lens for years (Cthulhu as an agent of chaos, destabilising capitalism and so on). Trillions of words after and too many drafts to still keep count of, I wasn't happy with it. It never finished clicking, as all brilliant articles do. But after meeting Mike, I was struck with another kind of revelation about Lovecraft's story.

'I know how we can get rid of him,' I said to Lì and Raúl during an Equality and Diversity meeting, AKA the Starving Postdocs Rebellion Group Chat. 'That old ruin on Klettr Hill. Wasn't that supposed to be an old Viking temple? We take him up there at night. Give him a good scare. A really good glancing-at-Cthulhu kind of scare.'

They laughed because they couldn't care less about Lovecraft, those two, but I knew he was the key to getting rid of our new nemesis. Mike wasn't like the other postdocs – Sharon, Dylan, Ned – he had the mental strength of someone on a permanent contract. He was disgustingly healthy (his commute to campus was also his morning run) and went to therapy (not because he needed it, he said, but to gain more self-awareness and enrich his life). He was nice to everyone, had a few boring friends, no partner, and no pets (not that we ever considered hurting anyone's pets, animals were always out of bounds).

'It's all in *The Call of Cthulhu*, come on,' I said to Lì and Raúl, trying to sell them on the idea. 'At some point, a bunch of underdogs, Black guys from the Caribbean, Portuguese immigrants and the like, decide to form a cult and start performing these rituals in a bog to invoke an ancient deity. Sure, we all know Lovecraft is racist as fuck, but my point is, that's us, right? The underdogs. The lesser kind of scholar in this department. Listen to this line,' I said, grabbing the book, '*what has risen may sink, and what has sunk may rise.* Sink, get it? Like in a bog. Klettr hill is very boggy. Perfect scenario to scare someone to death while the earth is swallowing them, literally.'

'Are you suggesting we act out a sort of pagan ritual? In a bog?' Lì was laughing so hard she cried.

'We won't need to do much, just take Mike to the worst parts of the bog at night, leave him there sinking, maybe for a whole night. That has to be traumatic if you don't know what's going on,' I said. 'And because he'll be so traumatised, he'll leave his job, he won't want to come back here ever again.'

'How would anyone get tricked to fall into a bog?' Lì said. 'He's not going to jump into it.'

'No, no, Lì, you're getting things wrong,' Raúl said. 'Just imagine. It's night-time. No moon in the sky. We get Mike high first. Mushrooms. Yeah, we get him super high and we drag our butts up the hill and provided we don't sink in the bogs too we could… wait, I've got it. A Cthulhu mask. I can make that. Lì, do they sell octopus in the Asian supermarket? I need tentacles.'

'Fuck off,' she said.

They started laughing again, convinced the plan had no legs. Me, I was already making up the steps in my head. Maybe reading *The Call of Cthulhu* hadn't given me all the inspiration for that brilliant article I'd hoped would save my already withering academic career. But it had for sure inspired me to advance it in a different way.

* * *

Our university was right in the centre of town, occupying several historical buildings, old churches, a sixteenth-century town hall, and even a little palace. The cobbled streets around it were always clean, framed by independent coffee houses, art galleries, second-hand bookshops, secret gardens and front yards full of flowers all year round.

But if you drove out of town, the sweet rolling hills became arid. Trees disappeared, and the few that remained rooted to the rocks were deformed by the wind. And above them all, a lugubrious black mound. Klettr Hill. It had a cursed shape that reminded me of a massive flying saucer looming over us all. When I first moved to this place, I found it upsetting, so I read everything I could find about it. It was considered a sacred place by prehistoric tribes and the Vikings had done ritual burials on its top. Later on, it was said to be home to the faeries. Even the Victorian landscape painters who were famous in this area hated the place and only produced a handful of postcards of it, mostly showing it at night. It was the perfect nest for a primordial god full of tentacles and claws.

* * *

We decided to go for drinks first, as the department did every Friday. By then, we had become good friends with Mike – which, I'll reiterate, wasn't all that difficult – and were sharing a small table with him, buying him pints with the excuse of it being my birthday. (It wasn't, I just said it was because I assumed that Mike would feel a bit more inclined to humour me.)

At midnight, I suggested a hike up Klettr Hill.

'Forget it,' Mike said as he came out of the pub with us. His cheeks were ripe roses and his eyes glittered. 'I'm done for the night. You youngsters go ahead.'

'No, no, no.' I locked my elbow in his and dragged him to Lì's car. 'You have to come. It's gorgeous up there. You can see so many stars.'

'But it's raining,' he said. 'Don't think you'll be seeing any stars up there tonight.'

'But it's so atmospheric,' I said. 'It's a special place. Did we ever tell you the story?'

Lì's tiny car was parked next to the pub. As dirty as ever.

'Klettr Hill has always been a sacred place in the area, there are the remains of an ancient Viking temple on top.'

'A Viking temple…?' Mike said.

Finally, I'd caught his attention.

'Never heard of that,' he added.

'Locals don't like tourists going up there.' Lì helped me, while she used actual keys to open the rusty car door.

'You need to see this, Mike,' Raúl said.

* * *

There was no traffic on the winding road up to the mound, and the small parking lot near the top was empty. My shoes got wet minutes after we started the ascent. Bog. Mud. Mike didn't complain, which I thought was a good sign.

'What exactly can you see from the temple at the top?' he said.

Raúl and Lì walked ahead of us. Lì had a torch we'd bought at the outdoors shop the week before.

'There are a few rocks scattered here and there. You can still see carvings in some of them.'

'I can't believe that people have just left it to rot like that if it's an ancient Viking temple.'

'This is the North. Heritage funding doesn't reach up this far,' I said. 'There's been some research done on the place, though. You can learn all about it at the museum in town.'

'Is there a museum in town?'

'Yeah, next to the supermarket and the Indian restaurant in the square. People forget about it. But there's quite a lot on Klettr Hill there. Bits and pieces they got from the Viking burials. And even before that. People worshipped some ancient deity from the bog, you know?'

The night was getting hot. It was an unusually warm March that year. Even the rain felt tepid, like soup. The air was charged: a storm was coming from the Atlantic. But we didn't know about it then; the weather forecast had failed to predict it.

Li's torch moved further and further away.

'Okay, this is it, I'm going down,' Mike said behind me.

'No, no.' I went back and grabbed his arm. 'It's totally worth it up there, you'll love to see the remains of the temple, I promise.'

'I'll come back another day, I'll—'

'No, it has to be now, come on.'

I pulled, and he must have felt something – the urgency in my voice, the dread, because if things didn't go according to the plan, everything would be lost. He let me drag him.

When we reached the top, the darkness had turned solid, like heavy iron planks. It was difficult to perceive depth in this state. Flickering lights in the distance. Town. Nearby cities along the coast. And beyond, sea turbines spinning, although we couldn't see them.

The top was also a treacherous bog. We sank more and more into it with every step.

Lì's torch was static now.

'Over here, over here,' she called us. Raúl too.

I knew the top of Klettr Hill well. I'd gone there a lot during my PhD, sometimes alone, sometimes with Raúl, who didn't mind hiking in the rain. The bog reminded me of Lincolnshire, of Dad and his farm, and even though I hated the place, with its misty days and infinite wetlands, a part of me still found it soothing. Plus, we had gone to Klettr Hill many times in the last weeks to get acquainted with the terrain. To mark all the possible routes for our plan and learn them by heart.

'Over here.'

Instead of following Lì's signs to the left, I went to the right, far from the deep end of the bog and its wet entrails. The dark sucked me in, so Mike didn't see my manoeuvre. Instead, he followed the light. He may have already been a bit frightened of me, but he still trusted Raúl and Lì.

We didn't see him fall into the depths of the bog, but we heard him. A loud shriek. Childish.

I kept walking to the right, away from his voice, sinking to my knees in mud, water and dead leaves but still able to move.

'Help me,' Mike screamed. 'Help me— there's water here— it's— it's cold, help…'

I reached Raúl and Lì on the drier side of the bog. We patted each other to confirm we were all fine. Lì kept her torch on.

'Help me, I'm here, here. I'm here, help— be quick— I'm sinking, I'm sinking…'

'Mike,' I shouted at him. 'It's fine, don't move too much, you'll be fine, it's the bog, you've fallen into it, but we're calling for help, don't worry.'

Lì switched off the torch. We didn't need it anymore, we knew the way down in the dark. Mike's screams sank like daggers in our backs but we didn't turn around, not once. Our plan was to leave him there all night. The bogs were not deep enough for him to drown, so he would simply be stuck there for a few hours. He was drunk. We were going to use that against him, to make everyone else believe that we'd never accompanied him up Klettr Hill. We'd admit talking about it, even driving to the parking lot in Lì's old car to watch the hill up close. Once there, Mike had insisted he wanted to go up and we hadn't been able to stop him. We couldn't have imagined the state of the bogs up there. It was a pretty good story.

By then, the wind had become stronger, and the rain harder. We had no idea that they were the precursors of one of the worst storms in years. A downpour of mythical proportions that would hit the area and cause floods and destruction like an evil god who had just been woken from his cursed dream. Getting down Klettr Hill, the rain wasn't too bad, and we were convinced that Mike would be safe. How many times did I have to do work around the farm when it was raining, hailing, or even snowing? You would have to be really weak to die because you were trapped in a bog during a storm. A storm that, sure, was intense, but didn't last more than a few hours. You could perhaps end up with a cold after that, pneumonia, even, if you were unlucky. But dying? Only someone really, really weak would die of that. (And how could we have thought Mike was weak when he was so energetic, running to work every morning, eating all that organic food he batch-cooked on Sundays?)

It wasn't Mike in my mind that night, as I trotted down Klettr Hill, but the grey bull Dad had in the farm once. How the bull got trapped in a bog, and his muscular body was so heavy we couldn't pull him out. We tried everything, Dad and I. Even the tractor. But the bull, which didn't stop bellowing, was too deep into the mud and the putrefied innards of the bog. In the end, Dad had to surrender to the fact that he'd lost a bull, and went back home. I stayed with the animal for a while. It was raining that night as well, and the bull bellowed his mouth raw, knowing full well he was doomed. It was a horrid vision. Reddened eyes and foamy mouth. A giant slowly dying, swallowed by something that seemed so gentle, so soft. A velvety carpet of ferns covering a mess of soil, dead plants, animal corpses, water.

It was things like that which made me loathe the work on the farm. I found it too cruel, too primitive. But maybe, I'm thinking now, maybe there was something that Dad and the rest of my family knew that I didn't, even though I was the first one to go out to university and get a PhD. I'm not saying this to justify what happened to Mike, but hear me out. Farmers have always made sacrifices to the gods to plead for good weather. In ancient times in Lincolnshire, they'd take things to the bog: food, trinkets, anything valuable. They'd even sacrifice other humans too, there's evidence of that, bog bodies, that's what archaeologists call them these days. Scholars don't agree but it seems pretty clear that these bodies could have also been bribes for the gods; pleas for sunny, benevolent summers and winters that didn't last too long. Good weather meant crops, crops meant survival.

Maybe we were not so different after all.

IN LOVING MEMORY
EWAN A. DOUGALL

Hell is living a life already half-forgotten.

In a quiet corner of the Headland, I sit on a bench warmed by the mid-June sun and struggle to recall why I ever left Hartlepool. A sea breeze breathes across immaculate flower beds surrounding the war memorial. Bright scents bring names and faces untethered from meaning. Snippets of conversations, of jokes and arguments, of someone else's family.

Everything I wanted was here and yet I've been away for longer than I can remember.

Twenty years?

Thirty?

I curl my hands into papery fists.

Manicured fingers touch my skin.

I snatch away as if from fire.

Two women crowd me: one on the bench at my side and the other standing. The woman next to me could be my Suzanne, right down to the chestnut hair threaded with veins of silver. Or Susie before she withered to grey nothing.

Did I imagine that?

'You're okay,' the woman coos in an unfamiliar – *Scottish?* – accent that must be a joke.

Her strange sense of humour is as unwelcome as her pity. 'Don't patronise me, Susie.'

A sigh. '*Lisa*, Dad.'

I peer over my glasses. Swallow a surge of embarrassment. My daughter, the teacher, not my wife, the accountant. If I'd been paying attention, I'd have noticed her nose isn't as upturned as her mother's.

If I'd been paying attention, she wouldn't have surprised me.

'Sorry, pet.' I offer an apologetic grimace.

'It's fine.' She's not a good liar. 'Did you hear what DCI Flood said?'

In front of me, a soft-featured woman clears her throat. I recognise the shadows beneath her glacial eyes as a carer's badge of office. Afternoon sunlight makes a halo of the hair spilling onto her shoulders. She fusses with it, her plain wedding band flashing.

I had forgotten all about her.

'What were you saying, love?' I cover my confusion with feigned nonchalance.

The women share a pointed look before Flood – *Fled? Flunk?* – flashes a customer service smile. 'Do you remember when we spoke on the phone last week, Mr Rivers?'

An innocent-sounding question asked in a local accent. Her tightening face betrays her anticipation.

I reach into my jacket for my notepad, a habit born from a career in policing. Notetaking helps with bouts of forgetfulness. 'What day?'

'Last Tuesday, the ninth.'

I flip back a couple of pages. My heart stutters as I scan the details. 'You found David Parker's body? You're sure it's him?'

She nods. 'His remains were found by a construction crew up the coast. They're clearing more of the Headland for housing. What was left of his warrant card was inside a heavy wool coat one of the older guys recognised.'

Stomach roiling, I sit back. The last honest police in Hartlepool, Parker was so proud of that coat. We laughed that he should be guarding a Soviet gulag, not arresting prozzies on Studley Road.

'Dad, are you okay?'

The voice echoes from three decades away. Rain and salt spray sting my cheeks but can't drive away the stench of decaying seaweed. Wet sand clumps beneath my fingernails as I dig a hole deep enough to bury my conscience in.

I squeeze my eyes against the memory.

'Mr Rivers?'

'I'm fine,' I croak, opening my eyes. Radiant summer dispels the bone-deep damp of that long ago beach.

The young detective hunkers down. 'This must be a shock.'

'Not really.' I take a steadying breath, check my notes. Her name is *Flood*. If I concentrate on that and don't think about Parker batting at my hands as I hold him under the waves of the North Sea, then she won't be able to read the guilt in my expression.

'No?' Her surprise sounds genuine enough.

'He's been missing for years, pet. I'd be more shocked if he was still alive.'

That has her nodding. 'But you thought it important enough to come all this way to speak to me in person.'

Of course it's important: I'm here to ensure they can't link me to Parker's murder.

'Do you know anything about this, Mr Rivers? Did DI Parker have any enemies? Anybody who would want to kill him?'

The first name I think of is the third man on the beach that night. *He* has to be dead, too. Nobody lives for long in his world, and he was getting on in years when I helped him roll Parker into that sandy grave.

What better way to keep my name out of the frame than to pin it on a dead man?

Still, his name chokes me. 'Ellis,' I manage. 'George Ellis.'

The detective straightens, lets out a low whistle. 'King George? Ran his outfit from Greatham? That's going back some.'

'Is he dead?' I try to keep the hope from my voice.

'Not so far, although he retired ages ago.'

My roaring pulse drowns everything else.

Ellis is alive. And I've just named him as a suspect in Parker's murder. Flood claims he's out of the game, but he'll remember how to deal with snitches.

I'm as dead as Parker.

I need to get out of Hartlepool.

Lisa shakes my arm. I flinch from the sudden touch. She nods at the other woman. 'Dad, Detective Flood asked you a question.'

'What?' I snap at the cop.

'Why would George Ellis want to kill DI Parker?'

Back then, just about every bizzy was on the take. Those padded envelopes handed over in darkened car parks by Ellis's goons kept Lisa in clothes some months.

But not stalwart Parker.

'I'm sure he had his reasons.'

I wish I remembered what they were. And why they were important enough for the King to be on the beach that night. Knowing might keep me alive.

Flood chews this over. 'Could it have anything to do with Parker's last case? The Baldwin kidnapping. You were with him on that, weren't you?'

Claire Baldwin, a Brownie snatched off the street.

'You'd have to ask Ellis,' I say, writing Claire's name and Jackson Street address in my pad beside a note that George Ellis is still alive. With luck, Flood will mistake my tremor for old age.

She pulls a face, thanks me for my time, and asks me not to leave town.

I start to tell her we're not staying when Susie – *Lisa!* – stands. 'Can I walk you to your car? Stay here, Dad,' she adds.

She doesn't wait for me to say no. They head for a dark blue hatchback. I crane my neck, scribble Flood's registration number, and pocket my notebook.

I sink onto the bench. The world recedes. Memories flash like lightning, but one stands out among the rest: Ellis's sour breath as he demands information about Claire Baldwin.

Why was he so interested?

I snap back to the present in a cold sweat.

Was he involved in her abduction? Was *I?* That would explain things.

Did Parker find out and pay for it with his life? And what happened to that little girl?

Bile burns my throat.

I scrawl a new mission for myself: *Find Claire Baldwin.*

Footsteps stop in front of me. The silhouette could be my wife. I snap my notebook closed, let her help me to my feet. She's taller than Susie.

'Lisa.'

'Hi, Dad.' She beams, like I'm a star pupil in her class. 'We've had enough excitement for today. C'mon, let's get you back.'

'Take me to Jackson Street.'

'What's on Jackson Street?' she asks, steering me towards a black estate car.

I can't say *Answers*, so I go with, 'Memories,' which means the same thing.

Argument flickers over Lisa's face, but a couple of minutes later, we're following a highlighted map on that fancy computer in the car's central console. I study St Hilda's Church and its haphazard cemetery. I should have buried Parker amid the worn gravestones: no property developer is going to landscape the Headland's sandstone heart any time soon.

The road curves. I catch glimpses of industrial docks between mismatched terraces. Distant clanging and klaxons skip across the water as stevedores disembowel vast container vessels, their skills passed down the generations. Steelworkers were the same, once upon a time. Before the foundries closed and filth like George Ellis rose to power.

We plunge inland. Hartlepool judders, my vivid memory warring against the town around us. Ghosts watch from the windows of a new college. I'd call the map a liar if not for the occasional recognisable landmark: Park Tower, with grimy white columns and stone balustrades unmolested, or All Saints Church atop a patch of grass not lost beneath concrete.

Yet progress halts at York Road. Here the worlds merge as we inch past streets clogged with parked vehicles. My driver draws up, kills the engine. 'Well, here we are: Jackson Street.'

I don't need her announcement. The same narrow terraces, overflowing drains, and uneven pavement. Only the names of local snitches I don't remember, daubed in crude graffiti across pebble-dashed walls, signal the passing of any time.

'This is where she lived.'

'Who?'

'The girl,' I say.

The woman's sigh comes from her boots. '*What* girl, Dad?'

I don't have time for this. 'Wait here.'

'Dad…!'

The closing of my door silences the rest of her outburst. I hobble in the direction of the Baldwin house, blinking against kaleidoscoping sunlight. Two shadows on the doorstep separate at my approach. The smaller slinks away towards Oxford Road.

The remaining figure adjusts the collar of his woollen overcoat. 'You took your time, Rivers.'

'Who was that?' I ask in a much younger man's voice.

'A john to see the Baldwin girl's mother,' Parker replies with a sneer.

'Guess he hadn't heard the news.' I knock.

The bed sheet hanging over the front window twitches. The door opens. A toddler frowns up at me with the unselfconscious inquisitiveness of childhood. I return his expression because Claire Baldwin doesn't have a brother. I twist to check with Parker that we've got the right address, but he's gone. In his place is a woman in a green sweater with anger in her eyes, so reminiscent of my wife.

I turn back to the boy, force my lips into a fatherly smile. 'I'm looking for Claire. Do you know her?'

Obsidian curls bounce as he shakes his head.

'What's your name?'

The boy glances back into the house. 'I'm not s'pposed to tell strangers.'

My joints shriek as I try to crouch. 'It's okay, son,' I whisper, 'I'm a policeman.'

'Mum!'

A hand on my shoulder. 'Dad! What the...' A pause as Lisa's eyes flick to the kid. 'What are you doing?'

The arrival of the boy's mother – all angles and cigarette smoke – silences any answer I had. She ushers her son inside. 'Fuck do you two want?'

Lisa gets between us. 'I'm sorry. My dad gets confused sometimes. He knocked your door by accident. Really sorry to bother you.'

'Get him fucking seen to.' The door starts to swing closed.

I shove past my daughter. 'I'm looking for Claire Baldwin!' I shout through the narrowing gap.

'Never heard of her.' The door slams shut. A key turns in the lock. Muffled yelling as she tells the boy to *never answer the fucking door!*

Lisa grips my elbow and marches me back to the car. She snaps my seat belt into place, ignoring my protestations, and storms around to the driver's side.

We sit in silence, going nowhere.

Gives me time to go over my notes, like I did all those years ago after Parker and I interviewed Claire's mother.

I dig out my pad. As I read, my nose twitches at the memory of acrid cigarette smoke.

'Do you mind?'

Parker takes a final draw on his gasper before tossing the butt out the driver's window. 'We should talk to the Brownie leader,' he says without taking his eyes off the Baldwin place.

'*Rhonda Lincoln*,' I read. At the top of the next page, my handwriting deteriorates into a mockery of itself, like an old man's writing. I must have been in a rush when I wrote *Claire Baldwin no longer lives at…* but that makes no sense. We were just there.

'Did you get the house number?'

The fake leather steering wheel squeaks under clenched fingers. 'I'm trying to be patient, Dad, I really am.'

A not-quite young woman – her face a stormfront – glares at me from Parker's seat.

My stomach pitches and rolls as the world pulses. 'Who…?'

'I'm not stupid. You think Claire Baldwin's kidnapping is related to your friend's murder, no matter what you told Detective Flood. So what are we doing here?'

I seize the name like a life raft, something to pin me to *now*. Flood, according to my notes, is investigating Parker's murder. 'I… I don't remember what happened to the girl.'

Another deliberate breath. 'You could have just asked Flood.'

My notes don't tell me why I didn't, but I can guess. Asking anything would have given the detective more reason to pry into my life. 'I didn't want to waste his time.'

'No, just mine.' She sounds weary, like she's had this thought a thousand times before. 'And Flood's a woman.'

I make a note as the engine hacks to life. We turn onto Oxford Road, then south on Catcote. So little has changed that I could be in Parker's clapped-out Ford.

Or a funereal Beemer. Ellis loved those black cars. '*Easier to clean*,' he liked to say. I would often find one waiting outside my house, Susie watching pale-faced from the front window. During the Baldwin case, Ellis wanted nightly updates at his Greatham home.

This car is black.

I never caught the model. Probably blindsided by the driver, who looks so much like Susie.

The next turn leads to the expressway and Greatham.

'Where are we going?'

My driver doesn't take her eyes off the car in front. 'Did you forget that, too?'

The turnoff approaches. She'll have to slow for the corner. I could jump. Liver spots pepper the hand that reaches for the door handle. Wild eyes amid a web of wrinkles appraise me from the wing mirror.

I hesitate.

'Dad?'

'I'm okay,' I tell my reflection.

We cruise through the junction, stay on Catcote. My heart rate refuses to slow as the road banks into an aspirational housing estate. Even with Ellis augmenting my salary, I couldn't afford one of these regimental semi-detached places with paved driveways.

My driver draws us up beside a silver Audi. A rangy man hoses it down, stepping out of our way. He waits for our engine to die before opening my door and extending a hand to help me out.

'How'd it go, Uncle Matt?' A local accent. Soft eyes so much like my brother's flick to my driver.

I climb out under my own steam. 'Fine, son.' My voice shakes with nerves.

'Dad,' my driver calls over the bonnet, 'do you want a cup of tea?'

Hired killers don't offer cuppas. Daughters do.

'Sure, pet.'

I let her lead me towards the house. Over her shoulder, she says, 'Andrew, I told the detective we'd stay in town for a couple days longer. Is that okay?'

'What are cousins for?' he says, returning to his cleaning.

Through a porch of frosted glass and mirrors, we enter the lounge. Lisa abandons me in an armchair on her way to the kitchen, returns moments later with a tray of steaming mugs. She places one on the end table beside me and heads outside with the others.

I open my notebook.

Find Claire Baldwin, my past self insists. A looping arrow connects her name to David Parker's. The arc is an unmistakable accusation.

No amount of tea can wash away the taste of guilt.

I lift my gaze from the page, find Andrew smiling at me from a holiday photograph, framed on the mantlepiece. A woman and two young boys stand around him.

The door opens. My daughter and nephew come back in, their voices dropping. I understand: Susie is dying, and Lisa's struggling. But it's my job as her father to protect her from the worst of it.

'We'll be okay, pet.'

Lisa ignores me. They vanish into the kitchen, where they can trust I won't hear.

Would she still ignore me if she knew about Parker?

I twist the notebook between gnarled fingers. I'm still gripping when another car pulls up. Andrew's wife and children flash unsure smiles as they enter. I grunt hello and tell her, 'They're in the kitchen talking about me.'

She shoos the boys into the garden and joins the party.

Let them fret.

I've got a missing girl to find.

But where to start?

I flip my notes open and start another read through, will some new piece of information to present itself, and try to picture the child. Dark hair and a yellow Brownie jumper smeared with dirt and oil. Blood, too. Livid stains on the bright fabric.

A fragment of a name accompanies the memory. *Lin-something-or-other. Lindon?*

Lincoln. Rhonda Lincoln.

Claire's Brownie leader. Why does her name conjure the reek of motor oil to clog my nose? The world falls away except for the sound of my nephew's kids bouncing a ball.

Thwack. Thwack. Thwack.

Wordless pleading punctuates each smack. I snap my head up.

The living room opens onto a mechanic's workshop. In the midst of half-assembled cars towers a monster in an overcoat. A whimpering man lies at his feet, feeble hands trying to ward off another vicious blow. Blood dribbles from his ruined face to splash his embroidered name patch: *Michael Lincoln, Owner.*

Cursing, I lurch to standing. 'What the hell is this?' My foot connects with a bottle. Dark liquid glugs across the cold floor.

Parker throws another punch for spite. 'You soft, Rivers?'

A hell of a thing to say to your murderer. 'You're going to kill him.'

'Who gives a shit?' He drops Lincoln to the floor, rounds on me. 'Arseholes like this are killing our town. They pay off cops and do what they want. Well, no more.' He slams a kick into Lincoln's gut.

'Lincoln works for the King,' I tell him. 'He'll carve strips off you if you break his toys.' Me more than Parker, because I let him.

I've never seen the predatory smirk creeping across Parker's mouth. 'If it gets his attention,' he hisses before asking Lincoln, 'Where's the Baldwin bairn?'

Fear and suspicion war in the beaten man's swollen eyes. 'Please...' he says through a mouth of broken teeth. Parker's ministrations give him the voice of a drowned man.

Parker aims another kick at his stomach. 'I found her Brownie neckerchief in one of your cars, you dirty bastard!' He flaps a yellow rag at Lincoln.

That's news to me. 'Parker, where did you get...?'

Footsteps behind.

I glance back, find my wife knitting her brows at me. 'Suzie, what are you doing here?'

'*Lisa*, Dad,' the woman snaps. Her face falls, consigning whatever she was going to say to nothingness. 'Detective Flood called.'

I don't know any Detective Flood. Must be new. 'I'm busy.' I turn back to...

A large window, beyond which two boys play football on a suburban lawn. I size up the room around me: a large living room, pictures on the wall, a couple of couches and an armchair. All innocent enough.

So why do I feel sick to my stomach?

Lisa guides me away from the window, steering me around a kicked cup and a puddle of tea, and into an armchair. I let her place me down and accept my notebook when she offers it.

'Detective Flood wants to speak to you in the morning.'

My gaze drifts to the window. Why, I can't say: not the boys playing outside, certainly. My shorthand holds no clues. For a brief moment, an ink smudge on my thumb reminds me of engine oil.

Or drying blood.

I should have worn gloves. Parker always wore gloves.

I need to wash up before anyone spots my guilt. 'Bathroom?'

Lisa points the way to a downstairs WC. Door bolted, I fill the porcelain sink. Water drips from the tap like blood from knuckles as I scrub at my papery skin. I lose myself in the cleaning, needing to remove any evidence of...

A knock startles me. 'Dad?'

Can't a man have any privacy? *'What?'*

'You've been in there for a while.'

'Give me a second.' I swallow a sigh, pull the plug, and dry my hands. The swirling water gurgles down the drain with a death rattle.

Lisa waits right outside. 'We thought you'd fallen in,' she says with humour that doesn't reach her eyes. 'I've asked you before not to lock the door.'

'I'm not a child.' I nod at her maroon jumper. 'You've changed.'

She pauses as if readying an answer, but opts instead for: 'Come on. Detective Flood is waiting.'

Flood…? 'I thought you said she was coming tomorrow.'

Without a word, my daughter ushers me into the living room.

Nothing has changed except everything. The furniture remains the same, but the light is wrong: slatted blinds ribbon bright daylight now streaming through the window. The boys no longer play in the garden and both Andrew's and his wife's cars are gone. A dark blue hatchback is bumped up on the pavement behind Lisa's wheels.

A tired-looking blonde woman sits on a sofa. The polite way she nurses a cup of tea tells me she's police. 'Everything alright?'

I grunt, shuffle around a small table adorned with mugs and a plate of biscuits to the armchair.

Flood waits for my daughter to settle on the couch beside her before fixing me with a frostbitten stare. 'I spoke to George Ellis.'

The name twists like a knife. How did she connect me to him? I cover my shock by choking down a biscuit, chase it with lukewarm tea, and nod for her to continue.

'He remembered Parker's disappearance.' She watches my face for any hint of deception, but I keep my fear down. 'He said you'd know more about it than he would.'

He wants me to dig my own grave. I reach for a shovel. 'Did he mention Michael Lincoln?'

The cup pauses partway to her lips. 'The mechanic?'

She knows her history. 'Lincoln's wife, the Baldwin girl's Brownie leader, worked as her husband's secretary. Together, they ran a car joint to launder money for Ellis. Parker found a Brownie neckerchief in one of Lincoln's private heaps when we stopped by for a chat with Rhonda.'

'Did Lincoln say anything?'

Hard to speak with a mouthful of blood and chipped teeth. 'Nothing useful.'

'The corruption in the police really rankled Parker, didn't it?' She phrases the statement like a question. We both know the answer.

'He didn't like it, no.'

'Did that affect his ability to do his job?'

I shrug. 'Not usually. But he went overboard with Lincoln. That was new.' *Murderous.*

'Enough for someone to want revenge?'

'You'd have to ask Lincoln.'

She sets her cup aside. 'He died. Around the time Parker went missing. Crashed his vehicle into a tree.'

Tea doesn't ease my dry throat. A car crash would be perfect cover for his injuries.

The detective – *Flood?* – writes something in her little book, pockets it. 'Just so I've got this straight: Parker discovered evidence linking Michael Lincoln to the Baldwin case. He was... overzealous in his questioning, possibly resulting in Lincoln looking for payback. Connecting dots, we could guess that Lincoln found and killed Parker before dying in a car accident. Is that about right?'

She's wrapped that up like a Christmas present.

I nod along, trying to figure her angle.

Flood stands. 'Then, all that's left is to thank you for your time, Mr Rivers. Mrs Henderson,' she adds, acknowledging Lisa with a bob of her head.

We all shake hands. Lisa escorts Flood to her car as I watch from the window. Another handshake, and the blue car pulls away.

With her departure, I'm in the clear. I make a note: *Michael Lincoln murdered David Parker*. It's a good lie. My failing memory might even let me believe it one day.

My stomach sinks as I skim back through the past couple of days. Parker's murder wasn't the only issue: I still don't know *why* I killed him. Or what happened to Claire Baldwin.

I can't leave without answers to either, but no amount of thinking will patch the missing memories.

There's only one person in Hartlepool who knows the answer to both.

A breakfast I don't remember eating threatens to surge up my throat. My knees buckle. I catch myself on the wooden windowsill and wonder if King George will be happy to see me.

Lisa re-enters the house. I school my roiling emotions, and scurry back to the armchair. She busies herself cleaning up plates and cups, returning from the kitchen with a fresh brew. 'We can think about going home tomorrow. I'll let Andrew know. And Dad? Your friend can rest easy now. You did him proud.' She flashes a sympathetic smile.

I grimace in agreement, cursing inside. Leaving tomorrow gives me no time to speak to Ellis. I need to see him today. But how? I can't drive Lisa's car and there's no chance in hell I want her anywhere near him, so she can't take me.

I've written Andrew's address in my notebook. Assuming Ellis hasn't relocated, he's a mile away. Close enough for a younger man to walk without concern: I'd be lucky to make it in under an hour. Long enough for my absence to be noticed.

Unless… if I wait until the house is asleep, sneak out like a teenager, I'll have all night to hike to Ellis' gaff, and get the truth from him. Take a leaf from Parker's book and beat it from him, if I have to.

Good plan. The trick is remembering it. I make a note in coded shorthand at the top of a fresh page to visit Ellis during the night.

My jittery anticipation lasts until Lisa suggests I put the book away, get myself ready, and go out for lunch. We spend the day in a town at once both comforting in its familiarity and off-putting in its otherness. Boarded windows war with busy shop fronts in my mind, unsure which is *now*, and which was *then*. A man bleeds in a doorway but nobody reacts. Kids run in front of the car without us slowing.

Am I a ghost in my own life?

Lunch comes and goes. Dinner too, I assume, as I regain myself in a strange bedroom. I'm dressed, sitting in a narrow chair beneath a darkened reading lamp, with my notebook open in my lap.

Visit Ellis.

An instruction I have no memory of writing.

My watch puts it a little after one. I could be in Greatham around two if I hurry.

I creep through the sleeping house and steal thief-like into the warm summer night. So different from the rain-battered night I last saw Ellis. Streetlights imitate baleful moonlight, bleaching the world to monochrome. On arthritic hips, I hobble between their halos on my way to devilry.

Visit Ellis.

The two-word mantra gets me out the deserted cul-de-sac and onto Catcote. I hide my face from the occasional passing car and make for the footpath to Stockton Road. Ellis ordered me to rough up a goon from a rival outfit on this path. My fists ache. I clench them, grit my teeth against the pain in my joints, and trudge on.

Crossing Stockton sends me tumbling through time. The same low houses behind the same low walls beside the same overgrown fields. My feet know the way.

Visit Ellis.

Bastard. He did this to me. Turned me into this husk of a man. Chased me from my home to spend a forgotten life in Glasgow.

My muscles scream as High Street gives way to Front. The road curves along a small park. I peel off down a tributary filled with drab, dark terraced houses.

At the very end of the row – separated from the rest of the world by a high wall and a higher fence – stands a single detached building. Lights burn in the ground-floor windows despite the hour. Not even in retirement does the business of pain and misery keep conventional hours.

Sweat sticks my shirt to my back. A fence post acts as a crutch to catch my breath.

Under a tangerine streetlight, I review my notes, reaffirm my purpose. Why did I kill Parker? Why was Ellis so interested in Claire Baldwin's disappearance? What did I do to that little girl?

Two dark cars on the driveway. I know without asking that the sleek Beemer belongs to Ellis: the hatchback is a mystery. Our confrontation will have an audience.

The door knocker thunders. I hold my breath as if to slow my galloping heart.

Footsteps on hardwood.

Light dawns across me. I blink against the glare until the silhouette in front of me resolves into a young woman. Recognition widens her ice-blue eyes at the same time as I realise I know her. Her name dances away, elusive.

'Mr Rivers?' Shock strangles her voice.

'I want to see him.'

She doesn't ask who. Instead, after a glance over my shoulder, she ushers me inside. Thirty years fall away as I cross the threshold. I wave away her needless directions and head through the first door on the right.

A couple of free-standing uplighters illuminate leather furniture in warm tones. The couches and wingback form a horseshoe around a decorative fireplace. Inlaid bookcases frame a desk facing the bay window, unread volumes within bathed in a laptop's pallid glow. No sign of the heavies who used to fill niches around the room.

I drop onto one of the couches and face a wizened corpse dozing in the wingback. King George drools in his sleep.

The blonde woman shakes him awake like a nursemaid. 'Dad, you've got a visitor.'

Dad? 'I didn't know he had kids.'

She shoots me a look but says nothing. Ellis comes to with a spluttering cough. 'What…?'

'Matthew Rivers is here.' His daughter steps aside for the old bastard to focus ice-chip eyes on me.

He repeats my name with the voice of an ashtray. 'You said he was senile.' He speaks to her but glares at me. 'Why is he here?'

Before his carer can answer, I say, 'We need to talk.'

Ellis's chuckle is a mocking wheeze. 'Do we?'

I take out my notebook, scan the pages. 'I let Detective Flood believe Michael Lincoln killed Parker all those years ago. We both know that's bullshit.'

At the mention of the police officer's name, father and daughter exchange a glance. The old man straightens. 'Sure it is, but who wants to take the fall for dealing with that fucking animal?'

His wording has me scratching my head.

Ellis continues: 'There are rules. You don't fuck with a man's family!' Spittle flies from his cracked lips.

His daughter raises a placatory hand. 'You'll give yourself a heart attack,' she tells him. Then, to me, 'What do you remember of the Baldwin case?'

No point in lying to them at this stage. 'Not much more than snippets. Visiting the mother on Jackson Street, Parker interrogating Lincoln in the garage. Updating you,' I say to Ellis, 'although I'll be damned if I know why.'

The King narrows his eyes. 'Because I fucking paid you to!'

Again, his daughter tries to calm him. 'Many people tried to hurt my dad, but nobody ever came after the King's family. Or the daughter he never admitted to.'

Thoughts pummel me like fists. I snatch at the first.

'You're her,' I breathe. 'Claire Baldwin.'

She offers a tired smile. 'Alive and well, thanks to you.'

Her father leans forward. 'And I repaid you for it. Write that in your wee book.' He jabs at my notes.

I ignore him. 'Where does Parker fit?'

Ellis bristles. 'You really are fucking senile. He fancied he could take on me and every wannabe gangster in Hartlepool. Going after Lincoln was his mistake.'

A yellow neckerchief swishes through my mind like a flag followed by a sense of confusion. *Where did you get that?* I had asked him.

My partner can't answer, but I can. 'Parker planted the Brownie neckie on Lincoln.'

Events play out behind my eyes like I remember them rather than imagining. Me, standing in front of Ellis in this room explaining Parker's erratic behaviour; both of us realising the truth. A good man gone bad: an honest man broken by the world around him.

Ellis grins at whatever he sees in my face. 'We went back to Lincoln, you and me, but he was gone. You spotted Parker's car on the lot, so we waited. A couple of hours later, here he comes walking back.'

'No Lincoln,' I say. 'He'd already dumped the body.'

The corpse nods. 'We followed him to a warehouse where he collected my Claire—' he reaches for her hand '—and down to the beach to drown her. Why, I never could guess.'

Again, I can. 'He'd crossed a line by killing Lincoln. He figured you wouldn't let that go, but he wasn't going to let you get him because of some low-level frontman. He wanted you to really hurt.'

The memory comes to me as though through gauze. Stalking across shadowed sand, the rain stinging my face, the tempestuous sea unable to cover the child's splashing as she struggles against the hulk above her.

Anger more ancient than time bubbles up. I'm not police: I'm nothing but fury snatching a rock as I rush to save a little girl. Satisfaction twists my face as I crack his skull. Ellis runs to check on his daughter, but I'm on my knees, my hands around Parker's throat.

I scream as I hold him beneath the waves. Unfelt rain stings my cheeks.

'Mr Rivers?'

Claire's voice brings me back to Ellis's front room. Tears run down my face like seawater as I kneel on the carpet.

She helps me to my feet, places me in a chair. 'It's okay, Mr Rivers. That's all in the past. Nobody will know the truth. But I'm sorry: I have to take this.' As she speaks, she takes my notebook, tears pages from it, and hands it back.

I reach for her. 'That detective… She might figure it out!'

The woman puts a hand on my wrinkled cheek. Her wedding band is cold against my skin. 'She did years ago. Before she joined the police to spite her father. Before she married and changed her name from Baldwin to Flood.'

Our eyes meet. 'You played me.'

Her smile is as kind as it is condescending. 'Your secret is safe.'

I try to hold onto everything she's telling me. But, as we head to her dark hatchback and to my own daughter, it's unravelling like frayed lace. By the time we reach Lisa, I've lost whatever it was I wanted to remember.

Lisa's anger is fleeting. She thanks the woman who says she found me wandering the streets. They seem to know one another, so I let them catch up. Hours pass. The sun rises, and with it, I come to a decision.

'I killed a good man once,' I tell them.

My daughter hugs me.

'That wasn't you, Dad,' she whispers.

Maybe she's right.

That was another man, who lived a life only half-remembered.

I let myself forget.

WHAT GETS FORGOTTEN
JOEY MᶜGARVEY

It was the hottest summer ever which is some kind of excuse. Everyone said how they were too tired to live. Maybe murder was in the air and me and Janet just breathed it in.

This was ages back of course. We were eight-going-on-nine and what I remember really is the ace times we had July through August. We'd built this den up in the bushes by the bankings and killed Mrs Eccles' cat called Tibby. Janet squashed it with this brick. We'd hung the cat up in the den for decoration or black magic or whatever. The flies got to it and it began to smell. I felt sorry when it was no longer pretty but Janet kept it there because she was really into how things decay.

The other kids wouldn't play with us because we were too rough or vicious or Janet was anyway. Me no one minded. I was quiet back then as was the world around me. Muffled I'd say now distant and glassy. Only Janet and me Mam ever made a real dent. Their voices just hit a pitch while others were bubbling mud.

The last week before school we spent in our back yard. Janet was brick-red and peeling and I was in this pink halter neck that showed off my tan. I think maybe the sun mussed up our heads but that's no excuse for what we did.

We decided to go for this walk to nowhere in particular the canal maybe or from back when there were mines these slack heaps that were slowly grassing over. Leon Swift was sitting on his garden path no one else about and asked if he could come with us. He was five years old and mardy with this enormous head and eyes always set to cry. Janet told him to fuck off and called him a little pisser but he came out his gate and followed us anyway so who's to blame there ay?

Janet and me walked off singing Raindops Are Falling on Me Head paying Leon no mind behind us stomping his tiny legs and wobbling his big fat head.

We ended up at St Maggie's not that we meant to. You set yourself loose and you can end up wherever but it was a place me and Janet went because no one else ever did. It was an old church older than anything and never used even on a Sunday.

Churches meant nothing to us then or now. At school Mrs Frame drew God on the blackboard. She said he was a bit like Santa Claus but with more to do. Janet said this was typical of grown-ups. They say they're looking out for you but they're always busy elsewhere. Janet didn't have the nicest Mam and any New Dad might change from week to week I'm not kidding.

Now what was best about Saint Maggie's was this big brick wall right round it. It was dead high and on top of it you could see the whole town the terraced streets stretched out and then the slack heaps and after that the two new motorways that wrapped around us where they said the countryside once was.

I loved climbing up on that wall with the breeze up my dress like a big tickly hand.

Why don't you come up here? I called down to Leon who sat on the grass fit to cry because the wall was too high. It was high for us. It must have been massive to a little tot.

Look at him Janet says kecking his pants.

I'm not says Leon voice thick with snot and tears he was holding back but not hard enough.

Then Janet goes dead soft and coos at him like a bird and winking at me so he can't quite see. Come up with us she was saying. It's lovely here. Come on.

He wanted to but daren't. It was me lured him up. Me he liked best because I wasn't Janet and had lovely hair long and loose about my face. It was me reached down. It was me said Come on Leon love. It was my hand he took not Janet's hand but it was the pair of us hauled him up.

I can see our house he goes all excited and brave now he's up with us and he lets go of me to point at where we live.

Where says Janet. I can't see.

There he says and lets go of her too or did she leave go of him or pull away so fast he lost his balance?

Whatever.

Who can say?

He wobbled leant forward flapped his arms corrected himself one way and then a bit too far the other way fell back and off the wall.

Look out I said.

It seemed an age before he hit the ground and his head struck the corner of a gravestone. Eliza Carlisle was the name on it. The dates I can't remember but wasn't that name dead old-worldy? I don't think I've ever met an Eliza not nowadays or even then.

Anyway there was Leon Swift lying dead but not greatly bleeding. Me and Janet were just you know not knowing what to do. We didn't panic though or go mad which I think is good. We sat on the wall looking down. Janet got out these Opal Fruits. She always had money for sweets from somewhere but never for new clothes or shoes. She offered me one but I said no. I must have been in shock.

What we going to do now I remember asking.

Janet chewed on a lime Opal Fruit and then said burn him.

She was thinking of their Samson who was dead. When it was a puppy she'd put it in the oven with a bowl of water so he could have one last drink and then she'd gone out to play with the heat on high. She came back expecting roast dog but the ten bob for the gas had run out.

He wasn't even warm.

Samson grew up to be a dog but got knocked down by a bike the year before. Some man who was one of her New Dads came out of Janet's house in his vest and underpants to pick it off the road its head all blood and its eyes like dusty glass.

This reminded us of Leon so we got down to get a proper look.

Janet prodded him with her foot. Then she put grass up his nose to check he was really dead. It's what doctors do she said. I didn't touch him. I thought death might be infectious and how would I explain that to my mam?

Let's leave him said Janet so we did but not until Janet unwrapped another Opal Fruit – a yellow one – and popped it in his open mouth.

Let him suck on that she said. This sounds quite cruel but then she added that it would give him something to do which I now think was quite caring.

This was a Friday and Leon wasn't instantly found. It was thought first he was missing and then stolen and so dead because the Moors Murderers happened not long before two towns further up.

Saturday Mam and Dad took me and my brothers over to Belle Vue where we went on Bobs Rollercoaster and fed carrots to Youki the tame giraffe. He had a purple tongue, the giraffe, not Bob. I don't know who Bob was.

Janet said she hung about Saint Maggie's by herself to see if anyone else turned up but no one did.

Sunday morning Leon was found. Maybe somebody still went to Mass at St Maggie's and spotted him. The word went everywhere. There were policemen going in and out the Swifts' house and grown-ups calling us in from playing out because we might be found dead next.

Sunday night Mam and Dad came up to say good night and how they loved me which I thought was quite nice. They did the same with my brothers even the bigger ones. Janet's mam never did stuff like hugs and whatever. She was never in. Some nights Janet had the run of the house and could do what she liked watch telly until it ended or walk about the streets eating chips.

Monday was our first day back at school and there was a policeman at assembly. Leon Swift who would have started there this very day was sadly dead. This we knew already. That was it. No counselling. No feely-feely stuff. Those things didn't exist back then. You shut up and moved on. Some kids did make a big show of being upset. Mariette Martin was one of them. Me and Janet decided to make even more show because after all Leon lived on our street. We were excused Music and Movement to go cry in the cloakroom.

Tuesday each year group in turn were lined up outside Mrs Earle's office where a policeman was asking questions. Our turn was just before the dinner bell and the whole class were concerned they'd run out of custard if we were kept any longer. The queue was alphabetical by the register so I was near the top while Janet being a Worswick was almost at the end.

Say nowt she whispered at me. Say you were with me sunning ourselves in your backyard which is true we were mostly.

So that's what I said. The policeman nodded. He'd probably heard much the same from others. It only took a few seconds and I was out and winking at Janet as I went past. She never did wink back.

Dinner went and there was custard but no Janet. Then it was Fractions and still no Janet but Mrs Earle came and she called me by full name. She told me to come this way. We goes back to her office where the policeman still was and Janet with him crying tears in both eyes so I was concerned.

I don't know if I was upset or frightened or what. This thick-necked policeman was mouthing words at me from under a moustache and I didn't know what was going on.

Have you been quite truthful he says.

I looked over and Janet wasn't looking back. I was on my own and scared.

You did see Leon Swift on Friday afternoon didn't you?

Yes I said and started crying too.

Now now don't upset yourself Mrs Earle says to me dead kind but only because the police were there. She was really a cow. She would cane you for walking on the grass instead of the path and for not pulling your socks up to your knees. She says just tell the nice policeman what he wants to hear.

I couldn't tell him anything. Words were gone from me. The nearest I could get were these giant-sized sobs that welled up in my throat like gobstoppers. Then the policeman said something that made the gobstoppers melt clean away.

Did you see this Black man in the park?

Janet sneaked me this look. It was a lowering of the lids as good as a nod of the head and I got the rest by telepathy. That was us back then. Close as breathing.

Yes I did. I saw him.

Did he have a car?

I nodded. I didn't know what colour. White sort of I think.

He nodded seemed pleased and wrote it down. And what did he look like?

Tall. With frizzy hair.

Did you see him approach Leon?

No but he was close by. Then inspired I added with a bag of sweets!

Did you see Leon get into the car?

I thought it safer to say no.

Why didn't you tell us this before?

I looked down at my new shoes for school and twisted the hem of my skirt and said I didn't want to get into trouble.

The policeman smiled and said we could both go.

It was nearly home time anyway and I wanted to know why Janet hadn't said what we planned.

I was at the end of the queue she said and got bored.

Nothing came of what was said anyway. For all our tears they didn't take us seriously. We were just kids. Girl ones at that. And Black men were not that many round our way. Word that one was seen about was common gossip but that was because me and Janet spread the rumour.

Someone had killed Leon Swift. No accident not a bit of it. He may have fallen off the wall himself but how did he get up there? Who put grass up his nose? Who left him unconscious to die of the cold? Apparently he wasn't quite dead when we left him. He died much later of exposure it's called which sounds rude. Nobody ever said a word about Opal Fruits.

I wasn't keen but Janet decided Mariette Martin would be next. Poor Mariette. I never liked her. She did ballet and tap and her ribbons always matched her socks. I wrote her a note on Janet's say-so about how I was tired of being friends with Janet and to meet me on the railway bankings outside school.

Tell her to tell no one Janet said and bring the note an'all so we can burn the evidence after.

Mariette didn't tell anyone and she did bring the note. We met up the railway bankings and sat deep in the shadowy bushes where I could hear Janet breathing behind us. First I acted shy and grateful and said the worst things about Janet. Then we talked about school and television and the boys she liked. Mariette was dead keen on boys. I was getting to like old Mariette. She was plump with freckles and hair she said was strawberry blonde but I couldn't see it.

Do you know Jeffrey Simner in the year above she asked as we knelt inside the shadowy bushes her spreading her good dress in a circle. I've been in the long grass with him she said. He showed me his and I showed him mine.

Janet leapt out from behind and grabbed Mariette by the throat and didn't leave go.

I didn't see the end of it. I ran off and hid until Janet was done and then I came back.

Mariette was dead. She looked it more than Leon. She was scratched and red about the throat with her tongue full out and where there should be white her eyes were bunny-rabbit pink. Much more like strawberry blonde should be.

Janet was rubbing her hands in her armpits sore from strangling Mariette. Now no one ever said Janet was pretty but I think she was with this wide triangle of a face she might grow into. I believe today she might be a most attractive lady.

What do we do now?

We mark her Janet said.

I just watched while Janet rolled up Mariette's jumper and carved a J on her belly but skin is tougher than you think and the scissors were nicked from school so very blunt. The J ended up looking more this wobbly crucifix. She also had a go at Mariette's hair not hacking at madly but like it was this privet she was trimming.

My mam's been with a Black man said Janet out of nowhere. He was at our house one night and when she was saying ta-ra at the door I went into her room and put me hands between the sheets and they were sticky with snot I think it was.

I wondered why anyone'd want to blow their noses in the bed sheets but my Mam was always saying how common Janet's mam was so a filthy habit like that was maybe what she meant. Janet's mam did have a lot of men. I think of the one who ran out onto the streets in his vest and underpants to pick up the dead dog. I wonder even now is that how he walked about the house in front of Janet not just her mam.

Janet's mam was a mam in name only. She once sold Janet to a neighbour who was off to Australia. She was stopped obviously but not before the neighbour bought Janet completely new clothes for the boat over. Also sometimes when Janet was away with me in the park or somewhere else her mam would tell everyone that Janet was dead run over by a truck just to get some sympathy or attention or whatever.

I hate her Janet said meaning her mam I think but it could have been Mariette lying dead between us. I hate everyone she said but you.

It was me who reminded her about the Opal Fruit. Our trademark. We left Mariette with a lime.

Murder made Janet thirsty and there was some dandelion and burdock at home. She liked her drinks gob-warm which wasn't a problem as there was no fridge. There wasn't much of anything at hers not even wallpaper in the hall.

It was five o'clock and her mam was just up and getting ready to go out. She'd run her shoes under the tap and was drying her nail varnish over the gas ring.

Where've you been you little bitch she asked.

In town you cow Janet answered back quick as anything.

They didn't find Mariette for a full week which surprised me as the railway's the first place I'd look. We did carry her right to the back of the bushes but all the same. When they did find Mariette Janet said to me I bet she ponged her. Otherwise we never talked about it.

The police never interviewed us one by one. They gave out questionnaires we did in class instead of Scripture. This time I made sure Janet and me answered the same. We put that we were in town but Janet got in trouble for drawing a dead Mariette on her questionnaire. Miss ripped it up and made her do another.

There was much more of a fuss than over Leon and at last they mentioned the Opal Fruits. The Opal Fruit Killer one paper said. I was almost proud but Janet took no pleasure in it.

She was acting very strange.

I found out from my mam and two of my brothers that Janet went round to Mariette Martin's house and Mrs Martin came to the door red-eyed and grieving as you would. Janet asked if Mariette was there. Mariette's dead love said Mrs Martin and Janet said she knew. She just wanted to see the corpse.

What was she was playing at? Going round to Mariette's like that and not taking or telling me.

There was more and worse.

She got suddenly and from out of nowhere friendly with Raymond Raddigan a lad in our class horrible with greasy hair and no shoulders. He had purple eczema on his hands and still did a blue band for the sky but there she was sitting next to him in Art laughing and chatting and dipping their brushes in each other's jam jar.

Home time Raymond Raddigan was going round the girls saying it was me killed Mariette and I knew Janet put him up to it.

I cried all the way home and when Mam came in from work I was too upset to even watch *Blue Peter*. Another of my brothers held me close and Mam stroked my face with her lovely hands and I remembered the breeze that had stroked me up and down that day on the wall at St Maggie's when Leon Swift died.

Why you so upset love Mam wanted to know. Is it because of Mariette? Was she a friend of yours?

I said yes because it was almost true and it had been nice sitting with her in the shadowy bushes the sun glowing at us through the branches and the weeds tall purple and gold.

Try to forget it Mam said. What's forgotten can't hurt you.

Dad and her took me to a Little Chef for consolation and double pancakes so I quite forgot about Janet and Raymond Raddigan and Mariette and Leon until night-time and I was in bed. I had the third smaller bedroom and all my brothers shared another one. It was late and well gone one and me who always slept was suddenly awake.

At first I wasn't sure but I heard this low moan from outside a moan the same shape as my name. Someone was calling me. I looked out the window onto the back yard but it was pitch black and then it was just Janet tiny in the middle and just her face but bright yellow in the so much dark. She'd lit a match and was holding it close to her. The match died and darkness swallowed her until she struck another match and then another. Darkness then light. Darkness then a flare of light and Janet smiling and the night again. With each flare she mouthed some words or other at me. I couldn't make them out but I blew back a kiss to let her know I understood. We were still best friends together.

Raymond Raddigan was not in school the next day but was found by lunchtime on the railway line strangled an orange Opal fruit in his mouth.

I couldn't look at Janet for shame.

How could she have been so stupid? Everyone had seen her walk off with Raymond Raddigan. How could she go and kill him like that alone?

All good things must end. Call it selfish but in the end I had to think of me. Love and loyalty must be forgotten. They'd burned bright within me for so long. Now they'd gone and spluttered out.

I still sat by her at a double desk. I didn't want to be suspicious. I was cold and stony while we wrote up our Daily Diary for Miss to read later. I wrote about how I was still upset about Mariette and how nice my mam and dad was and how we went to the Little Chef and had double pancakes the night before.

Janet leant over and told me to write she was there too.

Don't write pancakes for me she said. Say I had gammon and pineapple. That makes it more convincing.

I said I can't spell pineapple.

She said put gammon then or ham even.

Now Mam and Dad would never spend that money on gammon for Janet Worswick or even take her to a Little Chef but she was watching me dead hard so I wrote this and in a paragraph all on its own

janet worswick was with me at the little chef.

There I said and showed it her and she looked at me not like she owned me and I'd always do her bidding but like her big triangle face was lit with this smile just for me. We were best friends forever and forever amen it meant.

I thought right that's it that's me done.

Just before Miss collected our Diaries and Janet's attention was elsewhere with some scab on her wrist that needed picking

I put in my Daily Diary this great big NOT in capital letters just after the *was* and before the *with*. I sat back and waited for what would happen maybe nothing.

At the trial my word NOT was particularly praised. They said as how that one word severed the knot that bound this foolish impressionable girl me to this child monster for whom the word evil could have been freshly coined Janet.

My Daily Diary entry had intrigued Miss and then intrigued the police and next day I was called midmorning to come to Mrs Earle's office. I remember I got up from our desk without even looking at Janet Worswick next to me.

Of course in Mrs Earle's office there was the police with the moustache and a few others one of them a lady.

I cried and asked for Mam.

They rang her at work and she came straight away. She held my hand throughout and forgave me for what I'd done before I even said it. Mam could so easily forgive and forget.

I told the police everything. I left nothing out. I find that best when caught. I told how Janet had done this and that and how I'd stood back and let her.

The police were dead nice surprisingly but really it was a way to get more out of me. I cried bucket on bucket and the lady policewoman calmed me down with caramels.

You've been a bad girl a very bad girl said the only grumpy policeman. He didn't even have a uniform only a dusty suit and jam stains on his tie.

I know I said. I'll go to hell I will I said and I meant it too. We'd killed Leon Swift outside a church and surely God was watching. Then I told them where Janet hid the scissors she'd used on Mariette.

I cried some more after that. I did a lot of tears. You'd think I'd run out. Where do they come from so many tears? There must be a flood of them sloshing about waiting inside us happy to be let out. That's why we feel so good when our crying's done relaxed somehow at peace.

I expected to be taken to grown-up prison after that but Mam was allowed to take us home. We went in a police car and there was Dad and all my brothers waiting at the door. I was his poor little one his damaged princess he said. Naturally I cried some more. Mam packed a suitcase and until the trial we moved to Bolton and the West Pennines where my Aunty Mary rented a caravan.

Janet fared less well. She was taken straight to a cell and kept there through the night because her mam didn't turn up until the morning and then it was to get the front door key.

Janet was supposed to be the clever one but she didn't cry or act remotely sad. She accused the police of brainwashing her. She demanded a solicitor. She watched television. *Dixon of Dock Green. Z-Cars.* She knew her rights. She wasn't a bit girly or like a child and I do not think this was a helpful way to behave.

The trial was the first time we saw each other again. We weren't sat side by side in a dock but with our parents either side of court but I always knew what went on in her head.

I wore mostly navy blue to court which suited me and still does. Mam and Dad were tearful but also smart in clothes bought special from the Catalogue.

Janet didn't even wear a dress but slacks and a Batman T-shirt but at least they'd been ironed.

Janet's mam was there the nerve of her or she turned up most days anyway. She'd wear bright orange which goes with nothing and yellow shoes scuffed at the toe and sometimes this stupid blonde wig for whatever reason that kept slipping sideways. The trial you'd think was only ever about her. She'd tell the papers Jesus was only nailed to the cross while she was being hammered. It was described in court how she was a prostitute and she shouted out so what. She'd always hidden the whips and whatnots in the airing cupboard so Janet never saw.

I wasn't good in the witness box. I was shy and the judges and the people mumbled so much I'd just looked dumb or cried or both whereas Janet was well at home up there. She bandied words with the barristers even her own. She never smiled once. She didn't want anyone thinking she was happy or laughing inside. She described Mariette's death in such slow detail and extra loud for my benefit I feel. She added things that never happened such as how it were me that used the scissors on Mariette Martin and also on Raymond Raddigan even though I was never near Raymond Raddigan but at the Little Chef as can be proved. She didn't act sorry not one bit. No wonder she wasn't believed.

Mrs Earle came on and said I was a good girl but slow and weak. Dim and passive and faraway were other words she used and a dim bulb at best. Various experts came on and agreed with her. I was educationally subnormal. They said it smilingly so as not to hurt my feelings which was nice. I was the submissive partner clearly fragile and led astray and uncomprehending. In the end I was just a little girl and close to retarded at that.

Was Janet Worswick retarded Mrs Earle was asked.

Mrs Earle said oh no Janet Worswick was sharp as a tack. Janet Worswick was too clever by half.

Teachers never use clever as a compliment do they?

Janet Worswick was found guilty of manslaughter not murder because of her age and was indefinitely confined. She cried then. She cried buckets. Too late I thought.

The jury found me not guilty. I was thrilled but too busy crying to hear what else was said but you need to know was that judge was very anxious for my future. The trial done he said aloud he hoped nobody would discuss the matter further with me. It should be put behind me. It was all best forgotten which is what Mam most wanted.

It's true I was let off on account of being backward and susceptible but here's the thing I never was subnormal not one bit. Instead I was more than partially deaf. Being deaf doesn't mean you're thick. Beethoven was deaf so there you are. They found out I could never quite hear what anyone was saying. That's how I fell behind in class and in life generally missed the point. I was hearing the world as if from inside this dusty jar. I thought that was the way the world sounded. How was I to know? Aged eleven they found out and gave me a hearing aid a big boxy thing. The world rushed in on me loud and long. I had headaches for months from hearing so much noise and chatter until it settled down. I still turn mine off if I don't like what I'm hearing.

Janet still gets a mention now and then. Morrissey of The Smiths wrote a song about her something miserable you can't hum. She spent the rest of her childhood in reformatories and asylums probably until she was old enough for proper prison.

When she was nineteen she and this other girl broke out one weekend. They met two lads and spent the night with them in Rhyl. Sex took place or so the lads claimed. Someone took a snap of her being arrested. She'd had her teeth fixed and looked quite pretty so I was right about that triangle of a face. It was reported that she was led away crying so she must have learned how people soften if you give them a good weep.

And she's out now. Out for good. Been out since she was thirty. Out in the world growing old like me. She's been living somewhere doing something all of it anonymous. Under protection you see. Illegal to even find her. It's known she had one little girl so maybe more. There must be a fella with her too. Or fellas. Like her mam. The apple might not fall that far from the tree. Who can say? She might be a grandma by now. Imagine her near kiddies.

When there's an anniversary or a similar event or crime there's a fuss. Her story gets trotted out again but less and less. I think maybe the phone will ring and I'll be on the One Show telling all but there's never been a mention of me no photo no nothing. I'm not bitter.

Don't think I got off lightly. We had to move house me and Mam and Dad and every one of my brothers although they'd not been mixed up with anything wrong as far as anyone knew. Folk are very unforgiving. We moved several times in fact but each time it was to a bigger house in a quieter area and another brother got a room of his own so there's always an upside.

I'm coming up to sixty-one. I know! I've never wed not that means anything. People don't so much now do they? I've led a fullish life. I've medals for Latin-American dancing.

I go swimming weekly and do hot yoga. I've been in the management line of employment mostly at John Lewis and mostly Cheadle but I've done my time stacking the aisles in Lidl and behind the counter at Browns of Chester. I use my own name. Always have. I never mention the past and so I get forgotten. I might have told my husband if I had one because it'd be awful if he found out some other way. I'm seeing a man called Angus. We've no plans to wed and at weekends we go fly-fishing.

Truth to tell I miss her. Janet. Not her as such. I miss the things we did. Not the bad things obviously but never having again a close female friend. Other women want you to be confiding and that's not a skill of mine. Some days on the bus when it's raining and everybody thinks I'm the same as them wet and damp and no good for anything but a narrow life and whatever's ahead is always slightly less than I deserve I want to say out loud how I'm more than this but I hold my tongue while I'm trembling with I don't know rage inside. Nobody starts when they hear my name. Nobody looks at me and wonders.

Thirteen years ago I kid you not I served Mrs Swift Leon's mother. Little Leon would've been middle-aged by now head as big as ever and probably kiddies of his own and him doing God knows what. Anyway I sold his mother a microwave. Top of the range. A Whirlpool convection with grill function. I looked her straight in the eye and showed her its doings. She could have read my name on my lapel if she'd a mind. She didn't cotton on. They say grief's like a wheel. It goes round and round and never has a stop but she looked happy enough with her microwave.

I MUST GO DOWN
LAUREN ARCHER

Soft Lad was holding court again. Balanced unevenly on an upturned bottle crate, skinny arms aloft. The last of the strangled sun broke through the pub's net curtains, nature's spotlight casting him in a mad prophetic glow.

'You can divvy up the towns and cities of this isle into the territories of the pigeons, and those of the seagulls,' he told the small crowd gathered around him in our corner of the Lock and Quay, the room thick with ciggie smoke and intrigue. The end of days had already come, but the barflies still swarmed around their messiah.

'Manchester and Birmingham are undoubtedly pigeon turf.' At this, Soft Lad pointed a sweeping hand out of the window, where the idea of those hulking cities lay. The window was so flecked with rain that everything outside was mere memory. Shuttered shops and closed roads. A floodplain without adequate defences; a residential area with very few residents left.

I tuned out briefly and returned to find Soft Lad still banging on about pigeons. 'Scabby scavengers of the skies! Rifling through the remnants of discarded takeaway boxes, hoovering up wet chunks from puddles of congealed vomit.'

The crowd laughed and I laughed with them, even though I'd heard this particular speech countless times before. We were all just asteroids caught in Soft Lad's orbit, powerless to resist the force of his gravitational pull. His shoulder-length hair – still thick and shiny, even at our age and with his distinct lack of care for personal hygiene – tumbled down around his shoulders. The rollie dangling from between his thin lips sputtered ash as he spoke.

Next, he pointed down as though to hell itself, although I knew him well enough to know he was gesturing to the south. Those unfamiliar lands which, in the age of travel incursions and hard regional borders, may as well have been on the moon. 'Brighton and Bournemouth and the like,' I felt Soft Lad's crowd wince at these foreign names, 'belong to the gulls. Meaty, muscular beasts that grab your lunch soon as look at it, leave your kids gazing at upturned trays where their chips once lay.' There was a long pause, heavily pregnant, while Soft Lad worked his way up to the point.

'This patch of land, however, is contested ground.' At this, Soft Lad spread his arms wide once more to take in our domain, where the Mersey spills out into the Irish Sea. Perched precariously with his baggy grey sweater sleeves billowing like wings, Soft Lad looked every part the great bird himself. The albatross atop our storm-tossed ship.

'The centre is still riddled with pigeons. After all, there's as many discarded portions of cheesy chips and puddles of sick out there as any other urban sprawl,' At this, Soft Lad laughed, coughed, hacked up tarry phlegm, continued. 'Despite that, there's something undeniably coastal about this place that the gulls flock to. You see them hashing it out sometimes, the seagulls and the pigeons. Turf war on miniature scale. The birds can never seem to settle it, scrapping ceaselessly over this place which is neither land nor water but some spongy thing in-between.'

The crowd stirred in accordance. On this point I had to concede to Soft Lad, ever the stopped clock. Merseyside has always been a semiaquatic creature, amphibious if you will, and more so since the rain set in. One of Liverpool's major streets was once named Frog Lane after the colony which resided there, and I had no doubt they would soon return and reclaim it for their own.

Way out from the shops and multistorey car parks of the city centre, our patch is the most porous of all. The land of low, wide housing estates. Of corner shops and laundrettes and, inexplicably, an indoor paintball arena. To our west, the Mersey bleeds into the docks. To our east runs the leaking artery of the canal. Bootle – where we each were born, lived and now would likely die – stands between these twin water sources, planted in the middle like a manmade peninsula. Since the rain came, one or the other is usually flooded and so our ground is permanently waterlogged, our carpets in a perpetual state of recovery.

Behind Soft Lad's head, the pub's wood panelling and magnolia paint was mottled with dark mould. It festered in the corners and spread across the walls, sprouted up between the floor tiles and formed dark blooms in the grouting. There used to be big community get-togethers, when we'd spend a day cleaning the place up, spraying up clouds of bleach and scrubbing at the dank crevices. Then, a week later, the canal would burst its banks again, the pub would flood, and we'd be back to square one. For the last few years, we'd just left the water to it.

Soft Lad looked set to continue but then there was a popping sound above our heads and the pub went dark. I wouldn't have put it past him to fish out some candles and conclude his sermon in the flickering firelight, but the imminent absence of cold beer seemed to dissuade him. His crowd drank up glumly and dispersed, leaving just the four of us sat in the waning evening glow. Me, Soft Lad, Badger and Robbo. So entrenched were we in the fabric of our watering hole that the bones of each of our unremarkable arses were imprinted on our respective seats.

Soft Lad's place was at the head of the table, but he often neglected it in favour of some other pulpit from which to preach: balanced on a barstool or empty keg, even clambering onto the sticky surface of the table itself, his head grazing the low ceiling. Me and Badger, so called because a birth mark on the side of his head gave him a streak of white hair that ran through his otherwise straight black mop, sat to Soft Lad's left and right. I'd spent a lifetime trying to shed the image of Soft Lad's second- or even third-in-command, and never quite managed it, whereas Badger took to it happily. I'd also never managed to acquire a nickname – had always just been Ian – which tortured me for most of my youth but felt a welcome relief now, at an age when the bluster of a moniker turned to an indignity. Robbo, whose real name was Ray Carmichael Walker Robinson, had a seat at the other end of the table, facing Soft Lad. Only he never sat in it, largely because he'd been dead for more than thirty years. Top in his class at everything when we started, expelled before we got to our exams, in the ground not long after. We still ordered him a pint whenever we got them in.

At this point in proceedings, Soft Lad would usually try to lure us into a lock-in. He had one of those naturally persuasive faces. Green eyes that glittered with the promise of a never-ending evening; long, straight eyelashes like a Friesian cow. On this occasion, even he relented that the night had lost its mysticism and he gulped down the last of his ale, setting the empty glass down with a flourish.

At the pub door, we pulled on our waders and galoshes and headed out into the rain. It had started just over a decade ago. That summer, the bright, dry days just never came. April showers lingered well into June, into August. A long sunless summer spent sheltered under huge umbrellas in beer gardens, pasty limbs offered up in optimism. Then it was autumn again and the rain no longer felt misplaced. Bad summer, we told each other. Wettest on record. We thought we'd never see another like it, and each year since we've been proven wrong.

Although it was wet, it was still strangely warm. An almost tropical climate, deeply unnatural given our surroundings. This humidity sent greenery exploding out across the towpath. As we walked, we did so through a wild overgrowth. Rushes and reeds and ragged robins, pennywort and wild water lilies. The towpath was teeming with life, the green goose stools and watery white of seagull shit holding up Soft Lad's remarks about the region's varied avian inhabitants. I'd borrowed enough of his books to name nearly everything we shared our home with. I wasn't one for stories and poems like he was, but I liked the old hardback catalogues of plants and animals he'd amassed over the years. Liked to be able to tell a coot from a moorhen and share in the delight of spotting a grey heron.

The water was green too, with pondweed carpeting the stagnant surface. In the dying light, it turned the whole basin a nauseous, hungover hue. When we were kids, we were warned that the pondweed was the matted hair of Jenny Greenteeth. She who lurked beneath the water. Wide amphibious mouth full of razor blades and webbed claws of discarded syringes. Protruding ribs like the rusted wire of a sunken shopping trolley. She was born in the boggy moss pits over in Fazakerley, then when those were filled in, she had to find somewhere else to live. She'd not dare venture to the beaches of Crosby and Blundellsands, where a fleet of cast-iron statues stood sentinel. The city centre was out of bounds too, the Albert Dock too flush with tourists and gallerists and consumerists to make a peaceful lair for Jenny. So, she ended up with us. Wedged between the canal and the docks, Bootle is as sodden as they come; a natural destination for our Jen.

The wet dirt stink of the duckweed converged with the base scent of the towpath. A dizzying mixture of waste, both chemical and human, cut with the chewy stench of oil from the refinery. You'd take the dog out for a walk, hoping for some fresh air, and find yourself bent over retching by the time you reached the water's edge.

We'd all grown up together in the housing estate on the canal basin, where the towpath met its end. None of us had migrated far. Robbo drifted from sofa to sofa before meeting his untimely but inevitable end. Badger had a flat down towards the docks, where the views were better but the flooding was even worse. I stayed put in the same house I was raised in.

Soft Lad was the only adventurous one of us. He bought the boat back when there was still some novelty in water. He'd lived a suitably nomadic lifestyle for a while, mooring all over the North. Nearby in Litherland, then as far afield as Leeds for a spell, before drifting back down to the basin I could see from my kitchen. After a while, the water levels rose, most of the locks shut and he ended up stuck there. A private investment company bought the basin a few years back and tried to raise Soft Lad's rent to 'reflect the permanent residential status' of his vessel. True to form, he refused to pay. He was resolute in the face of bargaining and threats, lest 'soft' meaning overtly emotional be mistaken for 'soft' meaning weak-willed, the latter of which he was not.

Badger split off in the direction of the docks and me and Soft Lad rounded a corner toward the basin. As we did, a group of kids rushed past us on souped-up leccy bikes, DIY motors strapped to the crossbars. They rode two or three to a bike, puffing mechanically on brightly coloured vapes, locked in the ferocious rhythm of a shared lexicon. Their faces were obscured by black balaclavas, whether to keep the smell out or for some more nefarious purpose was hard to say.

'What do you reckon that lot are up to?' I asked.

Soft Lad shook his head, apparently disappointed by my cynicism. 'Delight and liberty, the simple creed of childhood,' he said, as though that was an answer to anything.

Before we parted ways, we vowed to meet up again at the weekend. Others said it was stupid, fishing when we were nearly underwater ourselves, but we clung to our rituals like barnacles to the hull of a wreck. Wednesday evenings spent in our corner of the pub, long Sunday mornings and afternoons casting lines into the water, sat on the same towpath we'd walked to school down some forty years before. Rods poised. Reels tensed. Sharing the quiet, a few tinnies and an old ice-cream tub full of maggots.

* * *

I started Sunday with the pointless ritual of showering and drying off, only to slip back out into the rain. Armful of rods and reels, tent stuffed into my backpack, chest waders rustling as I scooted out the door and onto the towpath in the inky spill of a summer sky caught between night-time and morning. The humidity hit me quick as the rain. My clothes were soaked through immediately and beneath them my skin was slick with sweat. What was left of my hair stuck to my forehead. My damp bones creaked.

The canal had breached its banks once more and flooded out across the towpath, sending roiling water spilling into the streets. On days like this, I believed in Jenny Greenteeth again. Saw her sprawled out, hogging the path, her reedy locks coiling around the railings and her silty bowels disgorged.

Fishing is for early risers, which is why Soft Lad was never much of a natural. You've got to get up early to catch anything decent. Before the runners and dog walkers and duck feeders and pram pushers, the Strava-mapping joggers and the gangs of balaclava-clad kids. I usually went around five and got our spot sorted, Badger joining mid-morning and Soft Lad whenever he fancied. I didn't mind. I liked to be the first there, before the sun came up, before anyone else's day had started.

That's why it was me who found him.

When I arrived at our spot, I came upon a squabble of gulls gathered around something, picking it apart between themselves. I shooed them away and they flew off in an agitation of white and grey. In their wake, they left a bloated thing. Skin stretched so taut as to be translucent, wafer thin. No longer able to conceal the rivulets of blue blood within. His face was badly bruised, his features distorted, but I still recognised him immediately. Soft Lad.

His flesh was tumefied, water bubbling up beneath the surface of his skin. Pondweed was caught in the strands of his long hair and my first illogical thought was that Jenny had taken him for her own. He certainly looked as if he belonged to another realm now, his poor putrefied body taken back by this place which, as he said, was neither land nor water but something else altogether.

What really got me was his hands. The skin was wrinkled, puckered up like he'd been in the bath too long. In places, the papery rind had whitened and lifted entirely off the pared flesh beneath.

For a while I just stood, looking down at him dumbly. I couldn't work out what to do. We didn't trust the bizzies. Never had, but even less so after the rain. The cities rose up and were beaten back down, us worst of all. So, I didn't call them. Instead, I set out my camping chair and sat with Soft Lad a while. The rain kept us both company, droplets hitting his broken face and clinging to the tips of his eyelashes. I thought of taking his hand in mine; it felt like the right thing to do, but the sight of his cockled flesh knocked me sick, and I couldn't bring myself to bridge the gap between us.

Badger arrived a few hours later.

He looked down at the distended mass by my feet and turned pale.

'Soft Lad,' he said.

It wasn't a question, but I nodded anyway.

'How?'

I shrugged.

Badger shook his head and unfurled his own camping chair, setting it up a little closer to mine than was usual. We sat in silence together – me, Badger and Soft Lad – until the morning drifted away from us, midday came around and Badger suggested the pub. I took the tent down and we wrapped Soft Lad up in it. We couldn't bear, I think, to go without him.

Soft Lad was a lithe, willowy sort of fella, so even with the bloating it wasn't difficult for the two of us to carry him. We gathered him up gently, the softness of him ossifying beneath our touch. The landlady, credit to her, said nothing as we lugged him in and convened in our corner. Soft Lad lay at our feet, his body wrapped in the tent's khaki polyester, and we both tried our best not to look at him. Staring instead out of the window at the familiar landscape that had now betrayed us. We knew every corner of the place, every gate and lock chamber. But somewhere along the way it had become hostile to us. To Soft Lad.

In the years since the rain started, the city had changed. People turned in on themselves, shut themselves off and hunkered down. There was talk of some taking lodge in the bricked-up tunnels and disused railway bridges beneath the city. Those whose homes had fallen victim to the floods, or who'd been driven out of them by rent increases from out-of-town developers. Liverpool was a city built on top of another city which was itself built on water. There were plenty of places to hide and plenty of reasons to take cover. The only question was where to start looking.

The hours came away from us in that corner as they had done many times before, but for once we didn't drink a drop. Instead, we sat and festered. A filmy melancholy grew over us like the cold skin that forms on a neglected cup of tea. Finally, Badger spoke.

'We've got to go there, Ian.'

I knew it, but hated to hear it still. We left without a word. Behind us, the landlady made her ardent protestations at the bundle we'd left behind, but we were too busy for niceties.

* * *

Soft Lad's boat was in a permanent state of disrepair, something always needing to be mended. Since the rain came, it had worsened still. The barge was barnacled; decorated with a mosaic of shell like the embroidered jacket of a Pearly King. You could have plucked an oyster off the side and shucked it, but nobody was so inclined. The wood was rotten and the paint peeling off so that the roses that once adorned the sides looked to have wilted and died. Worse than that, it had been vandalised. Scrawls of graffiti plastered the sides.

'Fucking kids,' I muttered. Badger nodded in accordance, making his way onto the boat and leaving me stood alone for a moment to examine the damage.

It was mostly the usual stuff – a menagerie of half-based insults and pornography – but one tag caught my eye. A huge symbol covering the cabin, sprayed in a bright postbox red. It was a perfect circle, with a triangle in the middle split in two by a vertical line. I had no idea what it was or what it meant, but it stood out among the filth and flirtation that surrounded it. I took a photo and stepped reluctantly aboard.

Badger, I think, had hoped there would be need to kick the door down, but found it already torn from its hinges. Inside, the place was a mess. Our boots landed on a carpet of smashed glass and ripped paper. I rifled through a pile at my feet, careful to avoid the upturned ashtray spilling out discarded ends. Scraps of old newspaper, tickets stubs from theatres and gig venues whose doors had been shut for years, an Asda receipt for a bottle of Buckfast and a six-pack of custard doughnuts. Nothing of any use, at least not that I could find.

The walls were still papered with postcards lifted from the gift shops of the Walker and the Tate, back when they were open to visitors. I pulled a couple down, remembering exhibitions Soft Lad had dragged me to, turning them over to examine the names. One, titled 'The Funeral of Shelley', was all darkness and misery, not the kind of thing I'd expect Soft Lad to like at all. Another, called simply 'Elaine', depicted an equally dreary scene: a cadaverous blonde clutching a lily as pale as her face. Shelley and Elaine sounded like women who'd have been mates with our mums as kids, and I wondered what possessed Soft Lad to collect portraits of them to decorate his narrow abode.

The place was stripped of anything of value – which, knowing Soft Lad, hadn't been much to begin with. All that was left were a handful of knickknacks and a few of his precious books. While Badger turned the place inside out, I ran a hand over the spines. *The Book of Trespass*; *The Lost Paths*; *The First-Time Forager*. Battered old collections of Keats, Coleridge and Blake.

I took down a small hardback titled *Poems of the Sea*. I recognised a few lines that Soft Lad had often quoted after hours, drunken and unprompted. I leafed through it, and it fell open on a verse:

'*I must go down to the seas again, to the vagrant gypsy life,*
To the gull's way and the whale's way where the wind's like a whetted knife.'

Somehow, those lines made Soft Lad's outlook make a bit more sense. I had never understood why he could not leave the waterways alone when the whole country was drowning, but perhaps he felt that same compulsion towards the channels, that same sense of *must*.

I wanted to pore over the words a little longer, but as I touched the pages in search of meaning, something crawled out from within the binding. It joined me for a moment on the page, before inching up my thumb. I flung the book down and the creature with it. It scuttled away, hoary armour glinting under the flicker of Soft Lad's single pendant bulb. I recognised it with a shudder. A silverfish. When I turned back to the shelf, I saw there were hundreds of the little bastards writhing in and out of the books so that the whole collection seemed to vibrate with invertebrate life. I suddenly felt I could hear scratching and scuttling all around me. I was anxious to leave. There wasn't much else to look at anyway, save for a pile of unpaid bills and rent arrears stamped in increasingly aggressive red. I grabbed a handful of envelopes and shoved them into the front pocket of my waders.

As we clambered out of the boat and back onto dryish land, we were met with the splutter of improvised motors. Moments later, that same horde of kids went by on their bikes. Featureless faces, beady eyes darting about from windows in walls of black polyester, leaving behind a trail of exhaust fumes and vape smoke.

We took off in something resembling a run, catching the last bike just before the bridge. Badger reached out and pulled a youth off it like plucking low-hanging fruit from a tree. He was greasy half-boy thing, head to toe in black. Badger gave him a little shove, sending him skidding on the wet cobbles, the aerated soles of his 110s nearly betraying him at the water's edge. The boy trembled. Badger was easily twice his size with a reputation for measured but prompt violence that still carried weight in our postcode.

'Take us to the rest,' Badger instructed. The boy nodded hurriedly.

We skirted along the towpath, each clutching a tight fistful of the youth's tracksuit top. As we crossed over the snake bridge, the youth tried to make a dash for it onto the Stanley Road. Before he could move a yard, Badger was on him, grappling his twiggy arm and pulling it up behind his back. The boy, rendered younger still in his pain and vulnerability, cried out and fell into line, his legs going limp. We dragged him down the slope and onto the path's continuation, past an old mattress and the skeleton of a discarded umbrella.

We rounded a blind corner and ducked under a bridge, sending a flock of nesting pigeons out of the rafters. That's when we saw them. Lined up in a row, dressed in black, blank eyes staring out from beneath their covered faces, misted by plumes of smoke. The one nearest held something in his right hand, and as he turned to face us, I felt sure the next sensation I would feel would be a bullet in my gut. Then the bubble-gum scented vapour around him dissipated and I saw he was holding not a gun, or a blade, but a fishing rod. They all were. Lines submerged in the still waters; old takeaway boxes full of writhing maggots at their feet.

'This what you lads have been doing down here?' Badger asked them.

They nodded, a row of balaclavas bobbing up and down.

I pulled out my phone and showed our captive the picture of Soft Lad's boat, hoping to prompt a confession. He shook his head and beckoned his mates over, each of whom looked at the photo in turn and showed no sign of recognition.

'I've seen that before,' said one. He pointed to the graffitied symbol that covered the side of the cabin. 'I've seen it in the tunnels.' He extended an arm to point further along the towpath, to the Litherland bridges and beyond.

Badger moved with a machine swiftness, tugging me by the arm and urging me on before the final syllable had exited the youth's mouth.

'The Half Miley,' he muttered, running a hand through his monochrome hair.

* * *

Beneath the spot where the canal crossed Marsh Lane ran an old railway tunnel we knew as the Half Miley. Us four played in the tunnel as kids, and although the new overgrowth made it harder for me to navigate, Badger thrashed his way through to one of the old entry points with ease. We stumbled across a dense wooded area, through puddles of water bright orange with rust. Squeezing through a gap in the warped fence posts, we dropped down into the tunnel's depths.

The bore was blanketed with a thick slurry of mud and dirty water nearly knee-deep. Again, I was thankful for my waders. The smell was claggy, the air thick with a rotten wetness that snuck up your nostrils and sat heavy on your tongue. As we traipsed through the thick sea, our phone torches found the flotsam and jetsam of discarded cider cans, nitrous oxide cannisters and torn open baggies. It was clear how the youths had become familiar with the tunnels, but we didn't have the heart to disapprove. We'd done the same in our own adolescence and we'd certainly had fewer sorrows to drown.

Gathered in one of the tunnel's small cubbies was a group of figures who had at one stage been human, but now resembled something else entirely. Their clothes were tattered and hung from their skeletal limbs by threads. They had the milky, pink-tinged skin of mole rats and red, shrunken eyes blinking horribly in the beams of our torches. I knew that these must be some of the people I'd heard about, who had taken to living beneath ground to escape the twin looming spectres of the rainfall and the rent.

Badger handed over his phone, showing them a photograph of us all from a night in the pub some months before, pointing out Soft Lad's face. They passed it between them, speaking amongst themselves. I couldn't make anything out. Grunts and chatters, something which sounded like a gasp but which could just have easily been a laugh. Whatever words they were using, the message was clear: they didn't know Soft Lad. One who seemed to be their leader handed the phone back to Badger. He had the stature of a child but the face of a wizened old man and was draped in ripped, muddied cloth. I thought for a moment that I saw a membrane of paper-thin skin webbing his bony fingers.

Around them, the high brick walls were covered in scrawling symbols of white. Crosses and arrows and wheels, seven-pointed stars and crudely rendered evil eyes. The youth was mistaken. These improvised hieroglyphs and runes did not match the symbol daubed on Soft Lad's boat. I turned the memory of it over in my mind. The careful arrangement of shapes had to mean something, but whatever way I looked at it I couldn't work out what. Only one thing was certain: wherever it pointed, it wasn't to the Half Miley.

We retreated back the way we'd come, our waders streaked with mud and dirty water. As we made our way out, we passed a fella heading in. A decidedly different sort to the fossorial folk we'd just left behind, with a cracking tan that suggested he alone had evaded the decade of shite weather everyone else had withered beneath. He brushed past us and caught Badger's eye for a moment longer than was custom.

'All sorts goes on down here,' Badger told me, managing a chuckle in spite of his grief. I didn't ask what he meant or how he knew. We were too long in the tooth for feigned ignorance.

Fed up of dead ends, we headed back onto the towpath and toward the basin, stopping in briefly at The Lock to retrieve Soft Lad before closing time. If we couldn't avenge our mate, we could at least give him a proper send-off.

* * *

Just as the apricot of evening was beginning to rot, there was a rare pause in the rain. We clambered aboard the boat's cabin and brought up Soft Lad's body, still wrapped in the flimsy material of the tent. Badger upended a jerry can of petrol as we disembarked, then lit a match and dropped it, sending up a wall of fire. We stood and watched as the flames ate Soft Lad. The air filled with the noxious smell of burning plastic and melting flesh. The shells that adorned the walls of the boat cracked and the wood darkened and fissured.

As I watched the boat turn to ash, I retrieved the bundle of damp letters from my pocket, pulling apart the first envelope to find what was within.

'Arrears of the deceased,' I read aloud. What followed was a series of numbers, the heights of which neither Soft Lad nor any of the rest of us could ever hope to reach. Each number corresponded to a service. *Rent, mooring, maintenance.* I looked at the smouldering barge. The peeling paint, the rotten wood. Nothing on board had been maintained for years. *Cruising license and associated fees. Insurance. Extermination.*

'Extermination?' I asked, remembering the writhing infestation of silverfish. I looked over to Badger. He shrugged.

Across the bottom of the letter was the name Aquatic Investment Organisation. The name rang a bell, and I remembered one of Soft Lad's drunken rants from a late night in The Lock, long after closing time. It was the name of the company that owned the canal basin, that set the rent increases which Soft Lad so diligently ignored. Beneath the name, the company logo. A merging of the initials AIO, rendered as a triangle within a circle, bisected with a single vertical line. I wanted to say something to Badger, but then he handed me a ceremonial ciggie, I had a puff and the words got stuck somewhere along the way.

Above us, the clouds darkened. The rain resumed first as a noncommittal wetness in the air, then thickened without remorse. It plummeted down, quenching the flames that licked Soft Lad's body. It wouldn't be long before he was returned to the waters he loved so dearly, to the clutches of old Jenny Greenteeth.

* * *

I lay awake that night, afraid to close my eyes and be haunted by dreams of Soft Lad beaten, bruised and burnt. I scrolled through the news on my phone, looking for something and nothing all at once. That's when I saw the headline. On some small North Yorkshire news site, not yet broken by the national press.

'Woman, 53, found dead in Skipton Wharf.'

My chest tightened. I sat up in bed and took my phone in both hands.

'Irene Mills, a local woman who lived on a narrow boat in Skipton Wharf, was found dead in the canal in the early hours of Sunday morning. Police are treating the case as suspicious due to the injuries sustained by Ms Mills prior to her death. A representative from Aquatic Investment Organisation, the company which manages the canal basin, said the firm was saddened to hear of the death of one of their longest standing residents.'

I stared at the words for a long time until my phone's light dimmed and I was left alone in the darkness. Outside, the rain hammered on my windowpanes like the staccato rap of wet knuckles. Like something waiting to be let in.

SAVING KENNY
STAN FENTON

Riley Morgan, the little shit, is hopping on his tiptoes. It's a decent tactic when someone's got a grip on your balls. *Not the twist, DC*, he whines. It's my signature move, and these fuckin wannabees, road men, scallies, whatever you call them, they're fuckin terrified of it. There's an urban myth going round – which I started – that I detached a lad's right nad who'd crossed me. Thing is, it's harder than you think, but these fuckers don't use their brains that often. Not for anything useful. So like I say, they're shit-scared of losing one of their precious bollocks. Some say I'd be edging towards doing society a favour. That's me: all heart.

What's your old fella's name, Riley? Wha, he says. *It's a simple enough question. What's your dad called? Tony, is it?* He stops hopping for a moment, but stays on his toes. *How did yous know? We were at St Pat's together. Tell him Deggsy Collins says hello, but it's Sergeant Collins to you. Call me DC one more time and I'll start twistin'. Go on lad, try me.* I move my hand as if I'm making the last turn to tighten a nut, which in a way I am, and his eyes flood with fear. *I won't D... er Sergeant Collins, straight up.* He's got one of those taches, our Riley, that when you see him from a distance, you can't be sure it's there. It's not much better at close quarters. Insubstantial, like the cocky fucker who's trying to grow it. His dad had one. That's how I clocked the family resemblance. That, the pointy nose and chin, and the fact he's all skin and bones. He's inherited his dad's good looks.

When did he move from Bootle? He didn't. I live with me ma. Figures. I wouldn't have put Tony down as one of those who'd get away. He had nothing about him except an attitude. Was all, like, the world owes me and I'm gonna take it. How did that work out, Tony? How do things look from your terrace in Bootle? *Came as far as Kirkhill to impregnate your mother, did he? How would I know,* sniffs Riley, and I can tell by the way he's sagging that the strength has gone out of his toes and he's going to faint any second. I relinquish my grip and pat him on the head, taking the opportunity to remove his cap and lash it behind me. Air Jordan: his gang's brand of choice. They might as well print a T-shirt saying *Stop and Search Me*.

Turn out your pockets, I tell him. *Ar ey,* he says, *don't be like that. Like what? A police officer? G'wed lad, turn em out.* Chewy, two phones, two vapes, and a small wad of notes. I press him against the wall and look right and left. The alley's clear because everyone scarpers when I make an appearance. Still, someone might be filming from a window, so I make a show of giving him the money back. I sniff the vapes. The one that stinks of weed goes in my back pocket. *Did you know this is illegal, Riley?* He shakes his head, and I half believe him. They think because it's a vape it's not the same as smoking it. Or maybe they don't care. I press a finger into his temple and push. *It fucks with your head, dickhead,* I tell him, *and if I catch you with one again, I'll nick you.* I won't – it's not worth the hassle – but he doesn't know that. The vape will go home with me to join the rest of them. I give them a wipe, leave them for a few hours, and we're good to go. I haven't had to buy one yet.

Why two phones, sunshine? One for your ma and one for your da? He looks at the floor. I press my palm into his chest. *What's your number?* He thinks about it for a moment, and then rattles one off. *Slow down,* I tell him, while I put his mobiles in my breast pockets. I take mine out and get him to repeat the number while I tap the screen. The one above my heart rings, so I give him it back. *This one locked,* I say, pointing to the other. *Yis,* he says. *Give it to me, then. 1-2-3-4.* I put the code in and sure enough, I'm in. *Fucking hell, Einstein, is that some sort of double bluff or are you as soft as you look?* He shrugs, and I get the feeling – call it experience, a copper's instinct, whatever – that the fight's gone out of him. I could crush him now, wring all the information he knows and doesn't know he knows out of him, but today I'm playing the long game. I want Riley Morgan to think he's got one over on me, but also remember how I had him by the balls. Besides, I've got his burner. I can get what I need in the five minutes he takes to shut it down; and the other thing is, I'm fairly sure that money isn't his. I'd rather have him on the street as an asset than get the shit kicked out of him by some goon who gives him the choice of exile or worse.

Right lad, on yer way. The moment he realises I'm letting him go, the pep returns to his step. He sticks his bony shoulders back and sniffs an unhealthy amount of snot to the back of his throat, the sound of which echoes off the bricks. He scrabbles on the floor for his cap, so I give him a boot up the arse for a laugh. *What d'yous do tha for,* he moans. *Shits and giggles, Riley, why the fuck not? Don't forget to say hello to your old man for me,* I shout after him. He's standing in the sun now, where the alley meets the street, and in that moment I'm struck by the framing. It would make a good photo. *I won't,* he shouts back, proper bold now he can make his escape. *Won't what? Forget to tell me da.* I wobble me legs so he can see. *I'm scared,* I yell, *fuckin brickin it. Yous fuckin should be,* he screams, *D fuckin C. He'll rip yer ead off.* A scrawny middle finger is Riley's parting shot. The way he says that, though, about telling his dad: maybe that twat Tony's got something going I didn't know about.

Back against the wall, I have a go at Riley's phone. A fucking Nokia. Takes a couple of minutes to remember how to use one, then I'm scrolling through his contacts. He's used first names or nicknames, and it doesn't take long to find the one I'm looking for. I hold my thumb over the name and wait. Three long rings. I picture him rocking back and forward in a tatty armchair, staring at a phone on a side table or little shelf. He answers. *Martin Hughes,* he says, and reels off his number. *Best not do that in future, Martin,* I tell him, *you never know who's calling. Martin Hughes,* he repeats, *who is calling please?* There's a tension in his voice, underneath that beautiful, but dangerous innocence that our Kenny has, too. *It's Derek Collins, Martin, we've met a few times at the day centre. I'm Kenneth's brother. Do you remember me?* Silence for a beat or two. *No, no, no,* he whispers, *I must not talk to the police. Yep, that's me, Martin, Sergeant Collins, but I'm Kenneth's brother. He told me he hasn't seen you for a while and he's worried. Sorry, Mr Sergeant Collins,* he says, *I'm not to talk to police. Are you on your own,* I ask, but he puts the phone down.

I've been looking out for Martin since his mum died last year. He's thirty, a year older than Kenny, but the pair of them are like kids. They'll trust anyone who makes nice with them. Riley and his scrotes will have watched to see if he had any other family or regular visitors. They'll have seen him getting the bus to the day centre Mondays and Thursdays. They might have followed him while he did his shopping – fuck, they might have seen him with our Kenny – and when the time came to find a new place, they'll have swarmed in, bees to a honey pot. They might have used a girl – another victim – to weasel their way in; and once they were in, he was screwed. His gaff will be a stash house, a place to deal, or a brothel. Christ, I hope it's just drugs. If the neighbours have noticed, they'll be too scared to say anything, and there's a good chance they've been threatened. It's happening everywhere, but I made a promise that I won't let it happen to our Kenny. His best friend is too close to home, and no one shits on my doorstep.

The toerags on my patch know better, but Riley Morgan's not part of any crew I've come across in Kirkhill. I'd clocked him of course, but not as part of any ongoing investigation, official or otherwise. These kids, though, one minute they're all noise and nuisance in parks and outside shops, and the next they're keeping watch while their mate sells baggies from a bike. They've spent their lives roaming the streets, in and out of the back alleys and passages. It's like they were in training. Unofficially, I don't object; but once they come close to defecating in my front garden, the gloves are off. I'd had my eye on Riley and his gobshite mates for a couple of months, on and off duty, waiting for the right moment to pull him aside and inform him of my rules and terms of business. One, no one under fifteen; two, no knives or guns; three, respect established boundaries; and four, pay your taxes on time. Things got urgent first thing this morning when I called round to our Kenny and he's heaving big, snotty sobs at his table.

What's up Ken, I asked him. *Has someone said something?* He banged his head against the tabletop and left it there. Wouldn't say nothing. *Come on, Kenny, you know I'll fix it if someone's upset you.* He thumped the table and started wailing. *Martin's gone.* I pulled out a chair, sat next to him and rubbed his back. *Martin, my friend. From the centre,* I said, *what do you mean he's gone?* He lifted his head and wiped his hand under his nose. *He doesn't come any more and Pauline says he doesn't answer his phone.* Pauline, who works at the centre, is my first port of call. *I can't give you his address,* she says. *But I'm a police officer. Then you know you have to go through the official channels. Data protection, sorry lovely. I did hear something, though.*

She's heard from someone who's heard from someone else – I get a lot of that – that Martin's been seen with a gang of kids, taking money out of the cash machine outside the Londis on Liverpool Road. That's another thing they do – relieve the poor bastards of their savings – and that's when my hackles go into overdrive. I should report this at HQ. I should leave it to plain clothes to get off their arses and make enquiries; but I don't want those knobheads vexing our Kenny. They're patronising enough with women and pensioners and besides, their success rate is not what you'd call stellar. So it's up to me to drive these cuckoos from the nest, off the books, so to speak. Hence my run-in with Morgan junior.

Martin and his mum are on the electoral roll, registered to vote at 17b Braddock Row on the Worthington Estate. It's where they house the pensioners, so I'm guessing the council doesn't know she's gone. Good for you, Martin. It's a sedate, friendly place where we don't have much cause to call, except when someone hasn't seen their neighbour for a couple of weeks and the smell under the door's attracting flies. Shame, then, if Riley Morgan has set up shop there. I clock his lookouts within two minutes of cruising by in the patrol car. They scatter into the stairwells or take off on electric bikes, into the passages where the car can't follow. I drive around the back of the estate, park up, and wait at the end of one of those passages. Lo and behold, a grey-tracksuited goon flashes past, not registering me in the shadows. He jams his brakes, pulls a skid and whoops, figuring, I guess, that he's escaped the clutches of the feds. He adjusts his Air Jordan cap, pulls a bundle of cash from his pocket and begins to count. Spotty face a picture of concentration, I let him finish his arithmetic before I step out and bang the heel of my hand into his solar plexus. He goes flying off the bike, but fair play to him, he holds the cash in the air as he hits the ground, and the bike falls on top of him. I grab the notes and flatten a boot onto his groin. *Thanks mate, that'll do for starters.* Shitbag has tears in his eyes. *The fuck are you doin,* he whimpers. *Cleaning the streets, scumbag. Better give that back,* he tries. I put more weight into my boot, and I can hear the air leave his chest. *Or what?* I let him consider my question, then push again. *I'm going to take my foot away,* I tell him, and *we're going to have a chat. Tell me what I want to know, and I might let you keep your bike.*

He won't name names, but his eyes are a dead giveaway. *You can tell Riley that Sergeant Collins says that when he comes by tomorrow, that flat better be empty of everyone except the person who should be living there. Touch a hair on that boy's head and I'll reciprocate.* He looks pained and puzzled. *Word too long for ya, fuckin dunce? Put it this way: hurt Martin, and I'll make you suffer.* He swings a leg over his bike and rises on the pedals. *You'll get yours,* he says, *fuckin DC.* I twitch my torso towards him, give him my best snarl. His feet come off the pedals as he thrashes at his bike. *Ey big man,* I shout after him, *ask your ma for a clean pair of skiddies when you get in.*

Back at the station, I call my old mate Mickey Fitz. He transferred to Bootle a while back, after a run-in with an inspector who wasn't a fan of old-fashioned policing. Turns out Riley's old man is very much on the radar. Tony Morgan's a nasty bastard, according to Mickey, and he's causing a lot of misery. Drugs and loansharking mostly, and there're rumours of a violent extortion racket. A real charmer. He's kept himself clean so far, which is a surprise. I wouldn't have credited him with the nous for that. I'm on my way out at the end of shift when Ally Blake, the titanic lump on our front desk, calls me over. *A couple of messages, Derek,* he says, *from the same person.* Loves calling me Derek, does Blakey. He knows how much it winds me up, but I won't let it show. *Anything urgent?* He shakes his head and sneers, like he can smell shit under his broken nose. *Not that special brother of yours, Derek. I'd have radioed if it was Kevin. Other than that, I'm not known for my mind reading skills. I have a name and a number if you can be bothered.* He waves a scrap of paper above his head, eyes returning to whatever he's reading under the counter. *It's*

Kenneth, as you well fucking know. And far as I'm aware, Blakey, the only skill you're known for is stuffing your face. How's the diet going? His grill goes purple, and he drops the paper onto the floor in front of the desk. *I have a thyroid problem.* I bend down for the paper and mutter *A fucking huge one*, making sure he can hear me. I stuff the paper into my jeans pocket and wait for him to buzz me out. *Goodnight Ally,* I say when the doors open. *Same time tomorrow, Deggsy,* he replies, *safe home.*

My phone pings when I'm getting into the car. It's from Kenny, in caps as usual: CHICKEN. I must get round to teaching him lower case. Good idea Ken, I think, patting the notes I've stashed in my waistband. Riley Morgan's henchman can pay for our tea. The rest of his dirty folding can go to a sports club or a day out for a seniors' group. Or my pension. Kenny's favourite chicken shop is on the parade on Pembroke Road. Finger Licken' Chick'n, it's called, an up yours to spelling, grammar, and the Colonel himself. Sami and Mo, who run the place, have this spicy rub that Kenny loves. I think it's Moroccan, and I won't deny it gets me salivating too. Mo raises a hand when I walk in and join the queue. *Ten minutes, Derek,* he says, *bucket for Kenny?* I put a thumb in the air and sit on a stool opposite a couple of kids who are all over each other. Judging by the state of their necks, they're at the love bite stage. How fucking romantic. The lad catches my eye and detaches his lips from his girlfriend's ear. *Fuck are you looking at, mate?* The girl jerks her head towards me, ready to join in, but she must recognise me. She whispers to her beau, and he lifts his palms. *Sorry bud,* he says. *If you've finished your meal,* I say between my teeth, *you can fuck off.* They slide off their stools and out of the door. *Just kids, Derek,* says Sami, coming over to clear their leftovers. We pump fists. *He started it,* I reply, *so I nipped it in the bud. Sorry, I don't mean to scare your customers. You don't,* says Sami, *not every time.*

We argue over whether I'll pay. I leave a twenty under a hot sauce bottle next to the till. *Give the change to charity,* I say, tucking the bucket under my arm. *God go with you,* Mo says, as he plunges a basket of wings into the fryer. *You too,* I answer, *although he might have given up on me.* Sami holds the door with his foot as his presses his hands together. *He doesn't give up on anyone,* he tells me. Yeah, right.

I put the bucket on the roof of the car while I fish the key fob from my pocket. He's a good lad, our Kenny, but he goes apeshit if his food's cold. I get in the car and send him a text: *ten minutes.* A reply comes through before I've started the motor: *no rush soon as you like,* winking face emoji. Kenny doesn't have the thumbs for a speedy response; he thinks emojis are the work of the devil; and it's in lower case. I feel a tightening under my bollocks, and my stomach flips for good measure, which means three things: that old copper's instinct again; the fight-or-flight response (very much the former in the case of yours truly) has been activated; and an idiot who has sworn to protect his brother has made a rookie error. I snatch the paper from my pocket and switch on the lights, cursing Blakey's handwriting. The numbers are obvious, but it takes a moment for the name to come into focus: Anthony fucking Morgan. If he's got Kenny, and anything happens to him, I'll never forgive myself. I put my foot to the floor.

Riley's scrolling through his mobile on Kenny's front wall, vape in his gob and a smirk on his chops. At the far end of the road, where the path runs parallel to the railway line, three more Air Jordan fans are arsing about under a streetlamp. The light's on in the downstairs front room, which Kenny doesn't use. Mum kept it for special guests, and we haven't got round to changing anything. I throw the car door open and stand over Riley, fists balled. *Alright DC? That chicken,* he asks, lips curling with the smirk. *Me belly thinks me throat's been cut.* He traces a finger from left ear to right. I think about launching him over the wall and stamping on his head, but if Riley is outside, pound to a penny his dad is sitting in our mam's house. There's a second of comfort that she's no longer with us, but Kenny… *Go on in,* Riley says, *he's waitin'. I'll mind yer car.*

I leg it up the path, all sorts of scenarios going through my head. Kenny tied to a chair, on the floor covered in blood, that kind of thing. I keep my cool in most situations, but where my brother's involved, stay out of my way. I try the handle, and the door opens. The chain is on the runner halfway down the hall. He tried at least, Kenny: he put it on the latch like I showed him, but they must have kicked it in. I turn left into the front room and there he is, Tony Morgan, still skinny as fuck with his nose and chin like a bastard woodpecker. In Mum's chair. Tracksuit bottoms, and a hoody, at his age. A scouse Peter Pan. Worst of all, he's chugging on a spliff in Mum's best room, flicking ash all over the place. *If yous have put any holes in that chair,* I tell him, *I'll do the same to your fuckin arm, burn for burn.* He flinches for a moment, then runs his shoe over a pile of ash. *Nice to see you, too, Derek. How long has it been?* I look about for signs of Kenny, a struggle, anything. *Not long enough,* I spit. *Where's me brother? Calm down,* he says, *and take a seat.* Him, offering me a seat, in my mother's house. I'm ready to tear him to pieces with my bare hands and fuck the consequences. *Where. Is. My. Brother?* He puts the spliff to his lips, inhales long and hard, and holds it in. I count to five before he bellows rancid smoke in my direction, like a gangster in a shit film.

You had a go at my lad, he says. *Put him up against a wall and took his phone. You made threats. Where's me brother,* I repeat. *One of his lads says you took my money and made more threats.* I stand and go to the window. Riley is peering into my car. I should have given him the bucket to keep him busy. *Know what a cuckoo is, Tony? Course I do,* he says, *it's that bird that lives in clocks.* I turn away from the window. *Funny guy,* I say. *D'yous know what else a cuckoo is?* He gets up and comes close, nose to pointy nose. *Sit down, Collins, like I told yer.* I count to ten and go back to the settee. He takes a mobile from a pocket, a Galaxy like the one I gave our Ken. He dials a number and sits next to me. He hands me the phone and says *Go on then, speak to your brother.* Kenny's on the screen, which is cracked in the same place as his. He loves that phone, and Morgan, the fucker, has taken it off him. I can't see any marks where he's been smacked, and as far as I can tell he hasn't been crying. *Alright Ken,* I say, *you okay there? You're in Mum's room,* he says. *We're not allowed in Mum's room. Special occasion,* I tell him, *we've got a visitor. Mr Morgan,* he says, *he was sorry about the chain. Where are you, Ken,* I say, *everything okay? Hungry,* he replies, *where's my chicken?* Morgan takes the phone from me and ends the call, but not before I've noticed the red plastic chair Kenny is sitting on.

St Pat's was closed years ago. I thought they'd knocked it down. I remember getting a hiding in assembly once. Mr Carney, the headmaster, had me face the wall while he banged on about how it didn't matter if a ball went on the roof, it was out of bounds at all times. The teachers were sitting on those red chairs, looking away while their boss gave me six of the best with a steel ruler, three on each calf. The school badge was painted on the bricks. I stared at it for twenty minutes through my tears. Funny how the memory works, because there it was, on the wall behind our Kenny.

Still in Bootle, I ask Morgan, who is back in Mum's chair. *Can't see any reason to move,* he says. *Happy where I am. Same house,* I ask. *Last four in the row,* he says. *Knocked them through. Not that you'd know from the front. Must be some council tax bill,* I say. *I get by,* he says. *Doin what? None of your business. Well,* I say, *given my profession and the fact that you've kidnapped me brother, it is my business.* He crosses one skinny leg over the other. *I suppose,* he says, *but it doesn't have to be. From what I hear, you don't mind lookin the other way, when the price is right. I know what they call you, Dirty Cop. The way I see it,* he continues, *I've already made a payment with what you took from that lad. Gave it to charity,* I tell him. *Oh aye,* he replies, *the type that begins at home. Tell you what we're gonna do: I'm gonna move Riley's lads out of that flat, and I'll bring your brother home. Very kind of you, I say,* gripping the cushion at my side. He points a dirty finger at me. *I haven't finished. I'm gonna do that, and you're gonna look the other way. No cuckooing,* I say, *not on my patch, and no guns. Your patch is it,* Morgan says. *I need to expand, and I like the look of Kirkhill. You're gonna smooth my way in. Anyone gives me trouble, and yous'll sort it out with your contacts. An obviously I won't get any hassle from the boys in blue. Goes without sayin,* I say, thinking I might as well play along while I work out what to do.

He fiddles with another phone and waits for an answer. *Bring it in,* he says. He takes two papers from a packet of Rizla in his hoody pocket, licks them along one edge and sticks them together. *Got a job for you,* he says without looking up. I hear a car pull up and a brief conversation. The car drives off, and moments later there's a knock on the front-room door. *Come in, lad,* says Morgan, as though it's his fuckin house. Riley enters, and hands a jiffy bag to his dad. *On your way, son,* says Morgan. *Go and sort out that thing we talked about. Okay,* says Riley. *You sure you wanna move…* Morgan raises a hand towards his lad. *I'm not tellin you twice,* he says. *Do what I said.* Riley cowers and backs away. *I'm on it, Dad,* he says, and disappears.

Fuckin kids, hey, he says to me. *Let's not pretend we're mates, Morgan,* I say back. *Tell me what you want and let's get on with it.* He throws the jiffy bag into my lap. *You're gonna deliver this for me. Where? I'll text you an address in the morning. You haven't got my number.* He waves Kenny's phone at me. *From your brother then, smartarse.* He points at the package. *Take that to the address, and when I hear it's been delivered, I'll bring him home.* I turn the jiffy bag over in my hand and give it a squeeze. Powder. *If anyone's hurt him, I'll come for you,* I tell him. *Well,* says Morgan, *you know where I live. Good luck with that. But I'm not an animal. No one's hurtin your Kenneth. Look, Derek, all I want is to go about me business.* I think he's about to give me the old we're-not-so-different-me-and-you-two-sides-of-the-same-coin shite, so I shut him up with a question. *What about the cuckoo? Riley's sortin it,* he says, *I wasn't happy with the arrangement anyway.* He finishes rolling his blunt, slips it behind his ear and gets to his feet. The cheeky get brushes the shite off his tracky bottoms, onto Mum's carpet. *I'll let you clear up,* he says. *Don't forget to leave yer phone on. You'll be hearing from me.* I jump up when he leaves, and go to the window. He climbs into a black Evoque at the end of the street, and that's me alone, making plans while I clean up.

First thing I do is go back to the chicken shop. They're closing up, but Sami comes outside when I thump on the door. *Need you to do me a solid,* I tell him. *Name it,* he says. I give him the lowdown and say I'll see him in the morning. After that I drive to Braddock Row where all is quiet. I creep up the stairwell, but there's no one about. I knock at 17b. A voice from behind the door tells me to go away, they've gone. *It's Derek Collins, Martin, you can let me in.* The door cracks open an inch, and Martin noses into the gap, opening up as soon as he sees it's me. *Come on, lad, we'll tidy up later. Get your coat and you can come to mine until we've got this sorted. Have you got a console,* he says. *Is Kenneth there? He will be,* I say, *one thing at a time.* I get him into the car and drive to my pad in Blundellsands. *You don't live here,* he says as we turn left off Crosby Road, *you live near Kenneth. I do sometimes, Martin, when I want some peace and quiet.* We cruise down College Road, past Marine's ground, over the bridge and right onto Warren Road. I feel like a different person whenever I come here, which is good because I wouldn't fit in otherwise. *Can we go see the sea,* Martin asks. I shake my head, pulling the car off the road. *Not yet. Let's get you settled, and then I'll go for Kenny. I'll set up the Switch, but you'll have to use headphones.*

Martin is happy as a pig in shit with Mario Kart, a can of Coke and a bag of Doritos. I hear Mum's voice telling me I should feed him properly, but it's the middle of the night, I'm not used to having guests, and there's the matter of my brother being in the clutches of low-rent hoodlums. I tell him not to answer the door to anyone, and he nods. Half an hour later I'm crouched behind a bush in the old playground at St Pat's. There's a red Astra, which you can't see from the road, parked by the fire doors at the side of the assembly hall. I crawl up to a window. There's only two of them with Kenny, who is lying on the floor, asleep on a shitty-looking duvet. They're sat on the plastic chairs, and one of them is also asleep by the looks of it. I leg it back to the car and open the boot, quiet as you like. I clip the standard-issue TASER to my belt, zip a cattle-prod into my bomber jacket, and grab the crowbar and a dozen cable ties. I run to the back of the school, praying that the drainpipe will hold my weight. I was about six stone lighter last time I used it to get on the roof, where I hadn't been looking for a ball like I told them. What I'd been interested in was the skylight over the staffroom. Always a nosey bugger, me, and light on my feet when it's needed. My calves throb with the memory of that beating, but the drainpipe holds up, and I'm forcing the skylight open quicker than Usain Bolt.

I get the one who isn't sleeping with the TASER. By the time the other one registers what's happening, the cattle prod ends his objections. Kenny sleeps through the action, but he's awake by the time Morgan's boys come to, tied to the old apparatus bars. I boot them both in the ribs, but Kenny tells me to stop. *Don't hurt my friends, Derek*, he says. *They're not your friends, Ken, they've been pretending.* He looks hurt and confused, but perks up when I tell him we're going to Blundellsands to see Martin. *Can we show him the Iron Men, Derek? When we've time, Ken. Come on, we'd better get moving.*

I just need to borrow these boys' phones. I lob them down a drain near the car.

I make a few calls when we get back to the flat. My colleagues aren't over the moon at being disturbed, but when I tell them about Kenny and how Morgan is making a move, they fall into line double quick. My brother and Martin are lost in Mario World when I leave, gobs orange with Dorito dust. I'm back in Kirkhill, outside the chicken shop, by the time the text comes through. I get out of the car, press the doorbell to the flat above, and wait for Sami. He appears in his Deliveroo gear, wheeling his bike in front of him. I give him the jiffy bag and the address. *Albert Road,* he says, *nice part of town. They've no respect for anything, Sami.* He shakes his head. I check my watch. *Thirty minutes,* I tell him. *Knock on the door, hand it over, and get the fuck out of there. My lot'll be there in thirty-five, so I want you three streets away by then. I ride like the wind,* he promises, and speeds off. I make another call about the shitheads at the school, then get in the car.

A few of the residents of Albert Road moan about their street being cordoned off until midday, but nobody complains about the arrest of the drug dealers who had moved into number seventeen when it had come up for rent. The raid on Tony Morgan's Bootle citadel is more complicated, but only crims get hurt. They nab the old man, but the kid is tucked up in bed somewhere in Kirkhill, far removed from the action. One for the future, is Riley. I don't get back to Blundellsands until late afternoon. Kenny and Martin haven't moved. They're sitting thigh to thigh, staring at my flat-screen, and I remember something I once read about how we come into this world unspoiled, from a shimmering past. What a load of shite. On the other hand, I doubt I'll see anything more beautiful for a while than two friends playing together, without a care in the world. I drag them from the sofa with the promise of chicken. We wander over to Burbo Bank, where Gormley's iron men stare out to sea, unmoved by the chaos. Me, I prefer to look left towards the city, where I do my best work.

ALGORRHYTHMIA
DAVID LAWRIE

i…

ok right.

picture it.

picture me hangin in them fotos you dont publish.

picture like a car park and the car parks made of dust an dirt. all this dust dirt flyin round everywhere cos its fuckin blowin a gale even though its maftin middle of summer like an all the dust dirts sticking to me. stickin to ma skin like some second fuckin skin.

an am drippin mega waves. an everythings all up in me like the past an shit cos i fuckin hate the summer always have. high winds blowin up ma skirt an that. like theres nothin nice about it fuckin hate it. everyone lovin it so hows it menna change when there aint nothin nice about it never was.

not gonna change now is it?

like in all them pictures an that. like in all the pictures with their bodies out.

all them stupid fuckin cars sitting round like stupid fuckin boy toys when they say we all gonna be fucked out the future anyway so whats the point?

whats the point?

picture it then.

picture all that.

picture me outside in ma scatty clothes like why the *fuck* would anyone wanna be outside with all this fuckin sweat an shit? even when i were a little girl i hated it. i were all like *nah mate* even fore the lads got in ma knickers ha. before they found the key. four-fucking-*teen* right an i were always gonna get it. like it were menna be.

an the lad goes off an leaves ya like when baby comes.

blah blah fuckin blah.

tryna get Moana on the tit when i barely had none.

an Elon...

Elon?

fuck.

Elon??

ha.

picture him draggin on his reins yeah. an am hangin off the back him like on them fuckin husky sleds. because i read about this forest yeah? like some enchanted forest swear down like they made it out of glass an shit. and its menna be like this fuckin enchanted forest an how this forest can give you a fuckin *spiritual* experience jus by *walkin* in it like. like it gets inside your lungs an shit. like it gets inside your mind. an i were readin bout all the benefits an shit like *natural mechanisms* or some shit an everythin was meshing up together like this proper fuckin web. like trees have fuckin whatsapp now?

not gonna lie. didnt even get it.

didnt get a word with Elon draggin on his reins like *nah mate whats all this fuckin green stuff mate?* tryna get him to read it on a screen like thought wed giv it a try yeah but he didnt wanna know cos of course it were like he knew it all already. *nah mate fuckin nah mate.* an i know he prolly did like. an i know it were like my fault anyway because i didnt pack the water an got a little shirty when he tipped over his yoghurt. cos it were hot like. only cos it were hot.

glass forests overrated anyway.

like two stars.

whats the glass forest like?

hot an a fuckin nightmare an theres glass an there are trees. what more you want?

an we got back to the car his buggy. an his buggy were in the boot i didn't even pack it. an i were all like *what the fuck?* fuck nos how it happened even now. Elon jerkin on his reins on ma shoulder like *Elon giz a fuckin sec mate* an him all like *nah mate* anyway an laughin all the time.

you know how he gets.

fuck me i were *wringin.*

coulda squeezed it outta me with no fuckin clue where Moana was at this point so i was all like screamin in the car park *Moana!! Moana!!* in the air cos she knows i fuckin hate it when she makes me raise my voice. fuckin makes all the people stare like when shes always wanderin off on her own with her nose in the air actin like she runs the joint.

MOANA!!

an i knew if she were round there she were ignorin me. what can you do? shes real pretty like they tell me. dont you think? dont you think shes pretty? pretty like her mother ha.

MOANA!?!

fuckin *hell.*

so wed lost her in the forest or some shit i dunno. an thats
when this fuckin smell comes creepin an i realise Elons doin
a massive shit inside his nappy. an i swear down he saves it
when were outside. like he saves it all up or summit. one of
his special fucking deliveries. SAS hand grenade *haymaker* or
summit comin right at me through ma nose an i can still taste
it if i think bout it. so i were in the fuckin car boot lookin for
the change bag with ma hands all gettin cut on bits of buggy
which is exactly why i didnt bring the cunt with stinky Elon
growlin down his reins at me like some fuckin xl bully an you
gotta laugh about it cos what else can ya do?

an thats when Moana went *boo!!* so i were all like *fuckin
hell Moana dont sneak up on me like that!* an she was all like
sorry muuu-uuumm! in that fuckin voice she does. *sorry muuu-
uuumm!* like its annoyin but its cute like an i were all like
where the fuck you been? an she did that thing with her eyes you
know? like *right here! all the fuckin time!* so i say to her *dont
swear young lady* an i dunno know where she gets it fuckin
mouth on her but *Elon needs a nappy change* an shes all like
bleurgh! an pretendin to be sick n that. an Elons had enough
at this point so hes yankin me towards toilet block an i only
got time to grab the change bag out the boot before were off
again at speed in an out of all them cars like he already knows
the way an im like *jesus christ Elon slow down a tad* cos i keep
skidding on the stones an shit. an i were tryna dig ma heels in
when we were comin on the toilet block cos it were this great
big fuckin *big* place that were cleaner than our flat an you
know it smelt amazin cos there were one of them automatic
fuckin freshener units spunkin an entire cart of whatever they
put in them things in the air an the babychanging cubicle had

one of them massive sliding door things like its off a train or summit so im sliding back this door pushin Elon in the space an its really fuckin tiny like theres no way on earth to do anything inside but you know when you got ta? had to get him on floor get his trousers down. an he starts flingin all these punches like hes in the fuckin Matrixxx an he clocks me on the jaw like so im really seein stars. an i manage to get his pants down round his ankles. standin there like some sad fuckin clown even though i need him on the ground an theres usually this move we do like some rugby tackle bullshit but there aint no room in that room for it so im puttin my foot behind him an tryna trip him over like in playground like. an he were fallin back an landin heavy on the floor so i were all like *oh my gosh you ok Elon?* but had to put all that to one side cos i were rummagin in the change bag with one of my other eight fuckin limbs that i swear you gotta have when this fuckin knockin woman on the door starts beatin on the door right when ive got him on the floor with a *knock knock* fuckin *knock!* an shes fuckin *canin* on the door like weve only just got in there so im tryna ignore the splittin headache formin in ma skull tryna do straps on his nappy when the voice comes like *hello?* an im all like *occ-u-par-doe!* obviously. but shes like *how long you gonna be?* so im all like *we only just got in here* cos we only fuckin did too an we were well within our limits right but then i cottoned on. an i were all like *Moana? that you?* cos now i think its Moana out the door doin one of her voices an that. one of them fuckin posh voices she does that isnt fucking real so im like *gotcha fuck! fuck off Moana!* but this womans voice is all like *pardon?* an i know its not Moana cos she wouldnt act like that.

an i were liftin Elons legs when he started unleashing this massive fucking tidal wave of diarrhoea shit everywhere like some mcdonalds milkshake machine sprayin everywhere an shit over everythin an its goin all over me an its runnin down ma arms an its all up on the walls you name it everythings getting covered. all this rankass fuckin shit fuckin sprayin *everywhere* so im scannin with my eyes literally for *anything* to help it an am huntin through the change bag with ma other fuckin limbs with Elon there cacklin his little chubby cheeks off like he planned it all along an prolly did the menace cos honestly you shoulda seen his fuckin *face!* me all gunged an shit like covered in it all like pluckin wipes from the dispenser tryna make some sort of barrier to block it all from comin shove it back into a corner an it took practically this whole tube of wipes to get it roped off an i just gotta leave it like that stinkin cos i gotta clean him up. gotta clean up all the shit hes made so im dusting round his asshole an his balls like swappin one nappy for another when the knockin comes again so im like *what the fuck is it this time?* cos i already told her i aint gonna be long an now theres all this shit to deal with so im like *you wanna fuckin deal with it bitch?* jus to myself like. posh fuckin cunt on the other side of the door like *knock knock* fuckin *knock* who she think she is? getting all up in my insides when am stretchin for the change bag an tuggin it towards me cross the shitty floor gettin hold of Elons wrists to try an guide him off the floor an hes really fuckin *graceful* for a change! shoulda seen him. an this knockin comes again. goin on an on an on at me but it stops right fuckin instant when i slide back the door back an im standin there covered in all this shit with cattleprod eyes an Elon on his reins gettin all feisty. an i tell you what. she backs right down. flinchin away from us like some terrified muthafucker like were alien or summit cos of Elon on his reins comin out at her like *you what mate?* an shes starin at him. fuckin starin all the time so im like *you wanna stop starin at him please?* an shes all like starin an starin. eyes out on stalks an she looks really fuckin pretty posh with this baby on her shoulder thats like dead to anythin happenin even though Elons shovin past an burstin from this tiny fuckin shit space so shes tryna back away when she nearly trips over this fuckin bench behind her so i already know shes not exactly steady on her feet but she wont stop starin at him so am like *you really wanna do that?* an she blinks an puts her head down. turns for the cubicle like an i really wanna get shot of her at this point so i let her fuckin go but i swear were halfway cross the car park when she says it. an i fuckin heard her say it. an she definitely said it. cos i heard it in that posh voice sayin *what kind of mother are you?* an i tell you that i heard it. i really fuckin heard it. so i were all like *nah mate* an spinnin all like *sorry mate?* an *you what mate??* same as anybody would be in that situation when she were tryna pull the door on me an i pushed it aside cos i were ragin an Elon was like *nah mate* but all i fuckin did i swear was give her a little shove. a little shove between the shoulder blades like it really wasnt nothing. it werent even fuckin hard. jus this tiny fuckin shove that makes her fall fuckin forwards like this massive fuckin overreaction with this fuckin fallin down. an i swear i saw her feet slip in all the shit. an goes down like a ton of bricks. fuckin cracks her skull off the side of the dispenser but it werent my fault. it werent my fault. it werent my fault at all cos i didnt shove her *that* hard an shes lyin on floor with

her face in Elons shit. an she aint fuckin movin. an the babys
rolled towards me. an its lyin in a bundle at my feet. lyin there
like this rubber fuckin baby so am all like *what the fuck mate?*
cos it wasnt even fuckin *real* an it werent even a hard shove
wasnt anything like.

an Elon starts laughin then cos of course hes always fuckin
laughin.

an i were nudgin the baby with ma foot. an i know you aint
menna touch other peoples kids but this baby were right there
not movin an i dont wanna make anythin worse with Elon
laughin all the time. pullin on his reins til were out of there.
back across the car park so i cant really do anythin bout it cos
what the fuck was i sposed to do? you know what Elons like.

an back at the car Moana was sittin there kickin her legs
round so i know summit was up with her cos thats what she
does. an i noticed she was wearin that dress ive told her not to
wear cos its too short on er an shes kickin all her legs round
an theres no shame in her. showin off to everyone with this
big fat fuckin grin.

an she turns to me

points the lens at ma face

an says *i saw what Elon did.*

an Elon aint happy bout it.

an all i wanna do is get in the car an drive away but Moanas
not havin any of that. an shes holdin the lens on Elon goin
i saw what you di-id! in thar fuckin singsong voice like shes
some fuckin horror film so im all like *cant this wait Moana?*
an shes like shakin her head goin *uh uh* with that grin an Elon
doesn't like it. doesnt wanna get in the car beside her an she
doesnt wanna be near Elon either cos Moanas got this lens

on him an her tongues pokin out an i swear i just wanna get them in the car go home so i can work out when he starts hittin her. an hes hittin her an hittin her. an all these hits are rainin down on her as she tries to hit him back even though she *knows* shes not allowed to do that not menna hit him are ya? an she knows it.

so im all like *Moana dont hit him!*

an shes hittin him an hittin him.

an im tryna pull her arm away when shes all like kickin all around an screamin. shes screamin an shes screamin screamin *i saw what you did!*

an Elons makin faces.

an hes laughin cos hes always laughin.

an theres all this dirt an glass an shit.

an am all gunked up in it all an *wringin.*

tryna hold myself back a bit cos i keep tryna tell her *it werent Elon it werent Elons fault*

an Moanas *screamin* at him like shes fuckin *lost* it

an i didnt have no choice

all i did was

like

give her a little slap

across the cheeks.

an i swear it wasnt hard.

cos i…

really do love her an shes…

shouldnt be hittin him like that.

cant be hittin him like that.

an she…

wouldnt stop screamin…

jus sittin there.

foldin her arms with this ice cold expression lookin up at me an...

sittin there an sittin there.

she doesnt make a sound.

an i dont make a sound.

an i wanna say somethin.

somethin like...

Elons laughin in the background.

an i can hear that baby cryin.

but all i did was like...

all i did was...

like...

youve seen the video havent you?

so you know all i did was like...

can i see her?

will you let me see her please?

please let me see her.

it werent a hard slap.

im sorry.

all i wanna do is see her.

please.

i get it now.

i get it why i shouldnt...

an i didnt touch the posh cunt.

please.

please.

i swear.

she slipped in Elons shit.

an she shouldnt have been...

anyway.

please!

you know how it happened.

picture it.

yeah.

picture like im hangin.

picture all the pictures.

please?

please.

wont you let me see her?

please?

fine.

dont picture it then.

picture whatever you want.

what do i care?

OFF BOOK
DAN HOWARTH

Whatever your level of fame, castings always happen in a shithole.
This is no different. Those awful circular LED lights blind me the
second I step in. The director and casting director are reduced to
silhouettes like crime victims interviewed on the news as we shake
hands and mutter greetings.

There's always tension in the air at these things, like a bar
before a brawl. I sit on a black leather couch opposite them both
and remove my jacket. Being certain of where it is at all times, my
leather holdall rests on the cushions next to me.

Once I've settled, the casting director leans forward and offers
me a copy of the script. Waving it away, I lean back, take a deep
breath.

'No, thank you. I'm off book for this.'

She sits back in her chair, back into the shadows which make it
impossible to ascertain if she's impressed or not.

'Go on then, kid,' she says. 'Show us what you've got.'

* * *

Dust dances in the light which arrows its way through the
curtains and straight onto my face, making me squint as I

open my eyes. Last night's excess beats a tribal rhythm on the inside of my skull as my phone buzzes over and over.

My hand gropes for the phone and a grunt of surprise escapes me when I see the name.

Arielle.

Answering on the third ring, I sit up as I answer, trying to keep the chemicals out of my words.

'Hello?'

'Gray, *darling*.' Every phone call from an agent includes the word 'darling', call it a cliché but they exist for a reason. 'It's been a while, hasn't it?'

Sixteen months, three weeks, and two days.

'A little bit, yeah. Are you okay?'

'Well, I've got you an audition.'

'An audition?' The word sits strange on my tongue. A remnant from another personality, another life.

'Yes. Now darling, listen closely. It's Film4. A northern production. They want you to read for them in about a month or so. Okay?'

'I'm sure I'll be free.'

'Me too.' A pause. When my usually breathless agent pauses, it only means something awful. 'Will you be...' Another pause. 'Sober?'

'I'm sober right now,' I lie.

'Yes, well, maybe more sober?'

'What's the part?'

'It's made for you. Everything you need is in the post. I'll tell them you'll be there.'

I pause now, awaiting the click of the call ending which always comes when Arielle's had her say, not when the conversation is over. A sigh from the other end.

'I'd say we're somewhere beyond the last chance saloon here, Gray. So, for the love of God, pull yourself together in the next few weeks. If you want to work again, it's this and only this.'

Click.

She's gone.

* * *

Arielle's parcel arrives the next day. It includes a handwritten letter from the director asking if I'm available. His writing sprawls across the page, as languid and one-paced as some of his films. His signature at the bottom a flourish of bent letter S's. Scott Simons. BAFTA winner. British working-class auteur.

Arielle's note is brief. It comes on a slip of paper headed with the logo of her firm – Hardcastle & Co. Her writing is curt, the words etched into the page.

DO WHATEVER IT TAKES.
Love,
A. xx

The bulk of the package is taken up by the book. Sliding it from the jiffy envelope, the quality of the cover material is tantalising to my touch, the Random House logo on the back lending it an air of legitimacy. The front cover is split into nine sections, each housing a sepia photograph of a person. The title is stamped in bold across this collage.

TALKING WITH THE DEAD: The True Story of Liam Ambrose – the Peninsula Killer, by Kate Langridge.

A press release slides from between the pages and into my hands. A black-and-white photograph of the author. Younger than me, maybe late twenties. Beneath are the usual blurbs from other authors and a synopsis.

In 1994, Liam Ambrose wreaked havoc on the Wirral peninsula. Men, women and children lived in fear for their lives. After dark, Ambrose would cruise for victims, picking up people at random to torture and eventually kill at his own leisure.

Talking with the Dead *is the blistering portrayal of time, place, and personality. Journalist Kate Langridge takes a deep dive into the community, the lives, and the events that shaped one of Britain's most heinous criminals.*

I drop onto the sofa, the book already open in my hands. The epigraph and dedication – the most intimate pages of the book – flying by me as I race to the story itself. Pages bend and curl beneath my touch as I read, as though I'm clinging onto them for dear life as the words rush on, bleeding into my consciousness. One chapter is gulped – two – more.

It's only when my back complains that I look up and see the sun is beating a retreat from the late afternoon sky and all the things I promised myself I'd do today – get as blitzed as possible as quickly as possible – have slid down my to-do list.

Getting up, I stretch, and pad into the kitchen of the studio apartment to boil the kettle. A cup of Earl Grey in hand, I sit back in the sofa, nestled amongst the cushions and blankets and discarded clothing, desperate to turn the page, to find out what happened next.

It doesn't occur to me at this point to think too deeply about who I'll be playing, where my character would fit into a dramatisation of these sickening events. All I can do is give myself to the story and see if this is something – anything – I can be a part of.

* * *

'You saw the note that came with the book, darling. Who else would you be playing?' Arielle's voice is a drawl.

'A policeman or a witness. It's been—'

'I know it's been a while, but your name is still kind of out there. The dying embers of your fame are waiting to be fanned. Read the book again. Put the work in. Get the job.' A pause as she sips a drink – probably a G&T, even before lunch. 'Got to go dear, next client and all that.'

A *click* and I'm plunged back into the silence of my apartment. No traffic outside. Neighbours all at work. Just me and the pages. I crack the spine, opening it on the photos in the centre of the book. Crisp black-and-white images, probably enhanced for publication. Victims smile demurely, blissfully unaware of the bloody, violent death awaiting them – in one case, barely a day later.

A man in his thirties wearing snooker-style spectacles holds the hand of a child, smiling outside a caravan. Dead two weeks later.

A young woman, frizzy red hair pulled back in a ponytail, smiles over a table of pint glasses in a pub beer garden. Dead within a month.

An elderly woman, the flash of the camera reflecting in her glasses. Her mouth a small circle of surprise. A lit cigarette in her right hand. Dead six weeks later.

A flick of the page. More victims. More snapshots of mundanity given a poignancy they don't deserve by the actions of one man.

And there he is.

Liam Ambrose.

He's a similar age to me but somehow old beyond his years. The photo is a candid from someone's birthday party. A silvery balloon bobs behind him. His tawny hair in an attempted side parting, too much gel reflected in the flash. The beginnings of a beard pockmark his face, the patches between goatee and sideburns yet to fully grow in. A checked shirt – badly ironed – tumbles over loose-fitting jeans. He is the embodiment of banality. Perhaps a trainee accountant or a supermarket shelf stacker. Someone you wouldn't remember if you fell over them. But therein lay his strength. Therein lay his power.

It's not hard to see why they want me for this role. If you squint, there's a vague resemblance. If I stopped the gym or the drugs or both. If I cut out the designer gear and the hundred-pound haircuts. If…

I lie back on the sofa, the book held up above my face, like when I read ghost stories as a child. I flick from page to page, skimming the captions below the photographs, but soaking in the details. Trying to put myself in that period. The early nineties. Merseyside. Rat-run terraced streets in Birkenhead. A remote beach at Thurstaston. Chocolate-box houses in Port Sunlight. Location didn't matter to him. Dropping the book, I dig out my phone. There's work to be done to get this role – to truly *know* this role. The peninsula is only forty minutes away. Looking at the ceiling I count down the hours since my last drink, since my last tab. Seven, eight, nine. It's enough. Surely.

Snatching up the book, I flip through for the reference I need. First, it's time to eat like a killer.

* * *

Bacon grease coats my fingers as they clench the steering wheel. The BMW is immaculate. It should be. This is the first time it's been out of the garage in months. After so long stuck in the apartment, the greenery of the trees, the swirl of gulls in the sky, even the undulations of the land open something up inside me which I'd long since pronounced dead.

Ploughing down the motorway, the peninsula passes me by. Place names familiar by sight but not through experience. Heswall – where some footballer once lived, a party there, perhaps? Tranmere Rovers – a bunch of try-hards in plain white. New Ferry. Rock Ferry. Cammell Laird. Maritime tradition left to rot like so many industries.

A left turn for Birkenhead. The town presenting itself slowly. Semi-detached houses on the outskirts giving way to lines of terraces and eventually lines of shops. A crossroads with a McDonald's on one corner, a pub – packed in the early Tuesday afternoon – on the other. Punters stagger between the two, intoxicated as much by grease as by booze. Rolled down shutters segment the streets between a bingo hall and shops with foreign goods spilling out through their doors.

Rolling the window down, I lean towards the air, eager to smell the place. The air is tainted, industrial, even now. As though the smog and chemicals still linger after all these years. Dust and dirt on the tip of my tongue as the car slides down the street, immaculate panelling reflecting the gawping faces of those on the pavement.

Deep breaths pull as much air as possible inside me, as though simply being here can bring a sense of knowledge to the place. A quick right turn into a multistorey car park and I'm out, on my feet and down the streets of the place. Kate Langridge's book weighs down my back pocket. A sinister Lonely Planet Guide. Shades on, nobody looks at me twice. Nobody's looked at me twice in a long time. Not since the papers stopped taking pictures of me outside clubs and bars.

So many empty units. So many closed shops. Banks shut down. Since when did they start doing that? A queue outside a baker's. Bronzed sausage rolls on display. Joining the queue, flicking through the book for the reference to Ambrose's favourite spot. It's elusive but something feels right. I order three; after all, Ambrose wasn't shy of the calories. The man behind the counter doesn't bat an eyelid.

Walking the streets, pastry flaking at the corners of my mouth. Hot, salted meat scalding me as I chew. I walk amongst the people – *his* people – some of them could've known him. Neighbours oblivious to his late-night movements. Classmates who never saw it coming. Colleagues as shocked as anyone else when the news hit, and Ambrose didn't turn up for his shift.

Sitting on a bench, chewing down the second of the three pastries, I leaf through the book as pigeons squabble at my feet. A woman pushes a pram with two children clinging to the side like desperate passengers on the last train out of a war zone. Their hard eyes rake across me. Rake across my book. The mother sneers, turns away, but I don't. I follow her, her thighs wobbling in Adidas tracksuit bottoms. Looking from a picture of Ambrose in the book to this woman and back again, trying to see her how he would've seen her. Trying to force his thoughts into my mind. Trying to channel his contempt for the living.

Anger constricts my chest burning hot and bright for an instant before fading away, like the heat of a pan dowsed with water, leaving me breathless and spent. How did he live like this? How did he spend every day in that frenzy – the fever of rage?

Forcing down the third roll, I walk the streets, back to the car park. Back to the sanctuary of my own vehicle, my own possessions. Every second spent in Liam Ambrose's mind is too long, too sinister. Yet there are levels and depths still left to plumb.

* * *

The glasses arrive in the post from a mail order site. They aren't the exact ones Ambrose used to wear but a similar enough facsimile. They sit strangely on my face, over my blotchy skin. After so long looking after myself, the carbs and saturated fat are eating me alive from the inside out. My hair is different now. The same side-parting Ambrose sported on his days in court. Unsettlingly precise. Often, when I'm reading my book – *the book* – my hands stray to my hair, the parting unfamiliar, to ensure it's not flopped back into its natural position. After a day or two, it doesn't. It learns to do as it is told, as we all do in the end. Adjusting my checked shirt, my overly baggy jeans, I admire myself from every angle.

'Getting there,' I tell my reflection. 'Getting there,' he says back.

* * *

Arielle doesn't tell me how she found the woman's details, mostly because I didn't ask. As an actor, I'm not a details man. I am where I need to be. I don't ask questions about sets and shots. I act. This is what I'm doing now as I swing the BMW onto the cramped driveway of Georgina Endsley's squat semi-detached.

Another check of my hair, another levelling of the glasses. A sharp knock. The door answered too quickly to reveal a short woman, paler than the photo in the book and twenty-odd years older. Sprouts of grey in her mousy hair, buzzing out of her head like electricity. Her green eyes widen. A hand moves towards her mouth before she stops herself.

'Georgina?' I say, an inflection of the local accent on my lips.

'Gray?' Her voice is a gasp. Those drawn-out vowels they have round here. 'You, you aren't what I expected.'

My chest swells at her words. She's as good as told me my work is paying off.

'Do you want to come in then?' she says, stepping to one side, inviting me to pass her.

A chemical reek of cleaning fluids lingers in the air. Juxtaposed to outside, everything is immaculate in here. Hoovered carpets, polished picture frames, a plumped-up couch in the living room. She brings in a tray of tea and biscuits. Drops into a seat opposite me and digs into the bourbons.

'How did he take his tea?' I ask. This mockery of an accent on my lips.

'You don't sound like you do on the TV. Suppose that's a good thing for you?' At my nod, she continues. 'Sweet. He liked a lot of sugar – in everything. Always had a biscuit with a brew. Every time.' A sip of her drink knocks the tremor from her voice. 'Never ate nothing healthy but never drank. *Never*. When we dated, my dad used to jip him for it. Didn't bother me back then. Thinking about it now, maybe the drink would've let it all out.'

'Secrets?'

'The real him. The one I never saw.'

Behind my glasses, my eyebrows raise.

She looks me up and down, looks away. 'I don't care what they wrote about me back then.' She inclines her head towards my copy of *Talking with the Dead*. 'Don't care what that snooty bitch writes about me now. I didn't know. Nobody fucking knew. That was the point. That's how he did it.'

'I'm not here to judge you. My agent tell you that?' She nods at my questions. 'I want to know what he was like to be around. I *need* to know.'

'His voice was deeper than yours. Just a touch. And he didn't open his mouth as much as you do.'

'How's this?'

'Less accent. But better.' She looks me up and down. 'Stand up.' Her eyes don't leave me as I get to my feet. 'Slouch a bit, bend your neck. He stood like he had the weight of the world on him. Probably all the fucking guilt. Yeah, let your arms hang more. Straighter. That's it. Yeah. His walk. Quite slow, he was a bit bent forward. That's it.'

She directs me round the coffee table, like a little boy trying on shoes with his mother. Her eyes glaze into a thousand-yard stare, as though she's seeing me and also seeing into me. After a few laps of the room, she gets up, tells me to wait where I am. Standing in this pose – *his* pose – arms by my sides, listening as she thuds about upstairs. She reappears with a dusty bottle in her hand. Garish gold glass.

'He always used to wear this on nights out. Probably the fanciest thing he owned.'

It's not a fragrance I'm familiar with. Some obscure Dolce & Gabbana line that's older than I am. Without asking, she sprays the bottle across my front. Chemicals on my tongue, acrid and wrong. Scent fills my nostrils, not unpleasant but not my taste.

She puts the bottle on the table and stands up straight. She barely makes it to my chin.

'Since it happened, nobody will look at me,' she whispers through static lips. 'Everyone finds out and won't meet my eye.' She steps closer, into my personal space. Her forehead is inches from my lips. 'Nobody has touched me since Liam. Not one person.' Her breathing deepens, corresponding with mine becoming shallow. 'And now you're here. It's like it's…' Her hand finds my crotch, rubbing at the front of my jeans. 'We never got the chance to say goodbye to each other.' She grips me, turns her face up to me. 'All I want is one last time.' She smashes her face into mine, her other hand searching the back of my head and pressing me into a kiss which is fury and loss and hunger. One-sided to begin with, but then I kiss her back.

'Come on,' she takes my hand. Drags me up the stairs.

Her bedroom curtains are closed, despite it being mid-afternoon. Half-light creeps through, painting the walls the same red as the material. A chest of drawers opposite her double bed. Framed pictures. Her and Liam – at parties, at home, at a christening. In the centre, a large picture of Liam in profile. Head and shoulders filling the shot. Those eyes stare out across the room.

Watching her.

Watching me.

She's at my clothes, ripping at her own. When I'm naked, she lies back on the bed. Her eyes drag over me. Seconds stretch out as she reaches for herself, her eyes combing every inch of me. Gooseflesh ripples across my body, a chill on my skin and in my soul. Then she's reaching for me. Pulling me down onto her.

'He used to call me his squeeze,' she mutters in my ear. 'Say it in his voice.'

I do as I'm told.

I do everything I'm told.

* * *

At her front door she pulls on my hand, stopping me from walking out. I turn back to her, unable to meet her eye. Her fingers on my chin, moving my face towards hers.

'I'm not a bad person,' she tells me. My gaze finds the doormat at her feet. 'And neither are you.'

I nod. Still unable to meet to look up. 'Did you know? About him?'

Something resembling a shrug. 'I didn't *not* know.'

'I need to leave. I've got some lines to run.'

'Remember what he said to me. Remember how he was with me. You'll get it if you want it enough.'

Another nod. Words have abandoned me. Breaking away from her grasp, I unlock the car. Its beep echoes off the neighbouring houses in the close. Dropping into the driver's seat, my body aches. Reversing off the driveway, one final look at her house. She doesn't wave from the door, just leans against the frame and watches me retreat. Shame rides shotgun as I weave through the streets towards the motorway. Yet, as the car slides from the slip road to the motorway, my eyes drift to the rear-view mirror. They don't see Gray McCabe anymore. Despite the bruises to my pride and the pain in my groin, they see someone altogether different.

* * *

It pays to be nice to people on set. You never know when they'll come back around. It's a small industry and people talk. Even on the worst days, the drink, the drugs, no matter how fucked up I'd been in the prep, I made a point of being polite to everyone. Even if my pleases and thank-yous were slurred, they were always noticed.

This guy, Andy, hooks me up. He'd been a stunt driver for me on some BBC production a few years back. Drivers aren't usually big drinkers, but we'd hit it off and he'd joined the list of very few people who've drunk me under the table. Some pub in Belfast if memory serves, although it often fails to deliver.

Andy slaps the metal side of the van twice, *bam bam*, as though petting it. 'This the one you wanted?'

Taking a step back, there's nothing to do but admire the beast. An old K-reg Ford Transit. White of course, the most inconspicuous colour, favoured by all manner of creeps and criminals. Rust tinges the wheel arches and bottom of the doors.

A nod of approval brings a smile to his face for the first time today.

'They used it on *The Bill* or some other show. Built in '92, still drives okay but don't thrash her. She's had a hard life.' He thrusts the keys into my hands. 'No fob, so they open by hand.' Andy leads me to the back of the van, watches as I slide the key in.

A crunch of rusty metal as the doors swing open to reveal a corrugated metal roof, the same white as the exterior paint. Chipboard covers the walls and floor. Watermarks litter the surface area. A smell of damp, of neglect. A nod of approval from me as the doors clang shut.

'You alright then, Gray? Been a little while.' He looks me up and down.

I say nothing, just waiting for his comment.

'You look a little... different...'

A loose smile on my face. My words come out in *his* voice. 'Just been working on a few things. Getting myself back on the horse, you know.'

Andy nods. 'Fancy that pint? Can do a few down the John Barleycorn later. You know how a few goes.' A smirk across his face, lighting his eyes.

'Got an audition coming up. Maybe after though, yeah?'

Liam never drank.

He nods, slower, sadder. 'Yeah. Maybe, eh?' A lick of his lips. 'I need this back in a few days. Look after her for me.' Pats me on the shoulder. 'She takes diesel. Don't forget.' He walks off, leaves me to get acquainted with my new ride.

His old ride.

The cabin of the van smells of damp wood. At the twist of the ignition, a roar bursts from it. Unlike the low rumble of a modern car this is throaty and raw – a nineties howl like Kurt Cobain. Vibrations tremor up through the driver's seat and steering wheel. We stay like that for a few seconds, man and machine joined as one. Then, throwing the van into gear with a satisfying crunch of the stick, we race out of the car park and onto the main road.

* * *

Liam Ambrose had a thing for hands. Fingers, thumbs. Something about the way they bend and change lit him up, turned him on. The pages of my new bible – *Talking with the Dead* – are littered with references to it. These phrases pop on the pages as I read in the car park, waiting for the shop to open. If the chapters are my gospels, these references are my psalms. My voice – *his* voice – cannot help but mutter the phrases from the book.

'Over forty fingers stuffed into a small leather bag.'

'A necklace of knuckle bones. Each one rubbed and worn.'

'A book of fingerprints of his victims. When officers finally arrested him, a strip search revealed ink stains on intimate parts of his body.'

The shopkeeper opens up as I watch on from my van. *His* van. A pall of gooseflesh ripples across my skin on the walk to the shop. A bell jangles on my entry and the man behind the counter double-takes me – once, twice, a hat-trick. My smile lights the corners of my mouth as I search for what I need.

Slapping two packets of rubber fingers down on the counter, I step back, keeping my face straight. My eyes meet those of the shopkeeper as they travel from the packets to me.

'Halloween was a few weeks back,' he says, holding the packets at arm's length as he scans them. 'Nine pounds.' He points to the digital display on the till like it would be invisible without his intervention.

A tattered ten folds itself between my fingers. He takes it from me, like he's picking up dogshit. Without looking up, he drops the change onto the counter and steps back as I collect it.

My fingers grip the door handle as he finds his voice again.

'Distasteful dressing like that round here. After what *he* did.' A sneer taints his face, his pale eyes even paler than before.

My fingers let go of the door handle and he audibly swallows at the sight of me stepping closer. The counter is on a pedestal but he's short enough for us to find ourselves at eye level. He shrinks back as I approach, some tatty costumes rustling in their bags as he leans back. Hands planted on the counter, I lean in. Teeth bared.

'You might want to keep your opinions to yourself, my friend. It'll be dark when you lock up tonight.'

A sound – something between words and a sob – makes its way out of him but I'm gone, the jangle of the bell ringing in my ears.

* * *

Two decades ago, nobody would've been out after dark. How quickly people forget. One moment the very thought of you is feared – revered in some circumstances – the next, people move on, and your name holds no more power than a whisper of breeze.

Men and women jog up and down the promenade. Somewhere beyond them, out in the black, the tide pummels the sea wall. Salt on my lips through the open window. A lonely gull squeals as I sit in the layby, engine off, lights off. My bible lies open on my lap, illuminated by the residual glow of the streetlights. It only shows the basic details of the photographs, but they're forever burned into my mind now. Even in pitch blackness, I could recall their every intricacy.

Feet pound the tarmac past the van. No one looks in. No one notices me sat here in the darkness. A few straggling runners in hi-vis and bright white trainers. An array of dog walkers – an elderly couple slanted into each other and a few solitary males walking dogs with more muscles than brains. My hands on the steering wheel. A tingle across my skin. Like those days you finish work early and head to the beer garden, the promise *anything* could happen.

The roar of the engine starting up doesn't draw a single eye. No attention. No nothing. The van slides down the street as though driving itself. Crawling down the main roads and then the lesser-known ones.

Time ticks on. Fewer people venture out. The hour doesn't matter. The opportunity will present itself sooner or later. They always do. So the bible tells me.

'Liam Ambrose was patience personified, a filthy Saint. No risks taken but high rewards gained. A temperament a poker player would've benefitted from. Taking time to weigh things up before striking. In an interview with the police after his arrest he referred

to "the ride", the way his stomach fell away as though on a roller coaster as he made his move.'

My fingers wind themselves round the steering wheel as the van takes me where I need to go. A quiet street at the edge of the town. A few houses facing out over wild fields of unkempt grass. A liminal space. A dividing line between urbanity and nature. Three streetlights. Five houses. A lone man walking down the pavement.

Pull in up ahead.

The van swings to a stop.

Open the back doors. Get the tyre iron and the jack. Get down on your knees on the pavement.

Concrete beneath my knees. A chill from the ground spreading up through me as he approaches.

Be ready. A final check. No one will see you here.

We're at the very end of the street now. At a corner before the road turns back on itself to another row of houses. Every window is set at an angle to where I am. There will be no witnesses.

The plod of footsteps coming closer. Ambling.

Kneeling down, the tools fan around me. All within touching distance.

You'll know. You always know.

The man enters my peripheral vision as I pretend to scramble at the tyre. In his fifties. Beer gut. Balding. He sees me, pauses.

'You alright there, pal?'

'Struggling,' I tell him. There is no recognition on his face, just a frown at the tyre beyond me. 'Never had to do it before.'

He looks around, up at the darkened sky and the closed curtains of the houses nearby. A deep sigh. 'I've got ten minutes, let me have a look.'

You've got him.

Stepping back out of the way, he shuffles past me, squats down. He tilts his head this way and that, assessing the angle. 'Okay, looks straightforward.' He reaches out without looking round. 'Pass me the wrench, you've got to get nuts off the wheel before you jack it up, that's where you're going wrong.'

You know—

The advice dies mid-sentence. Liam is not talking to me. He *is* me. The iron is weighty to my touch, a satisfying balance to the tool. Like a baseball player, I step into the swing, bringing it through at waist height, straight into the man's temple. He doesn't see it coming. He takes it like a champ. A long blink before his eyes close properly and he keels over onto his side in silence.

Nobody tells you about the dead weight of someone unconscious. The upper body strength needed to move them anywhere. The burgers and pasties of the last few weeks take their toll. A lack of arm days in the gym count against me. By the time he's in the back of the van with all the tools, sweat runs down my sides, my glasses askew on my nose.

You'll know the place when you see it.

'I know the place now,' I growl to Liam. Hoisting myself into the driver's seat, wrenching the ignition, the van roars away.

* * *

The van judders over the divots of the potato field. Lights off to hide us from onlookers. Vibrations shake my hands as I open the back doors. He's still out cold, spreadeagled on the chipboard floor, moonlight giving me the most tantalising glimpse.

The leather bag in my hand is full of blades. Each one carefully sourced not only to protect my anonymity but to replicate Liam's original kit as closely as possible. Wooden-handled butcher's tools. Blades built to last, sharpened to the hilt. In my right hand, a pair of bolt cutters. Liam's preference for taking his signature – digits. The handle is light in my hand, poor quality metal painted red to match Liam's pair.

The man doesn't stir as I pull myself up into the back and the suspension drops beneath my weight. Clicking on the internal light and pulling the doors shut behind me, I get to work.

* * *

'I have to say,' the director pipes up as I'm zoning out, letting Liam's voice guide my performance, 'you look a lot different to how I remembered you. This outfit, it's quite something.'

The silhouette of the casting director nods next to the director, her ponytail bobbing along. 'Superb effort.'

'Wow us,' the director says. 'Hit us with your best.'

I clear my throat, blocking out Liam's voice as he tells me what to do, what to say. I've been through his domain, worked my way through his instructions and his world. Now he's in mine.

'Everything they said about me was true,' I say in Liam's voice. 'All those news articles about me, all those facts they gleaned from

neighbours and friends, they nailed the "how" of the situation. But they never understood the "why".'

Pages flip in a torrent of A4. Frowns obscured by the strange lighting.

'I can't find that in the script,' the director says.

Ignoring him, I hoist my bag from the sofa and place it on the table between us. The sound of the zip is too loud, almost comical in the silence of the room. Upending it, I tip them all onto the table. The fingers. Some of them bounce from the tabletop onto the floor at their feet. Others roll over and over before falling still. In the harsh, ultra-HD light of the room, the dirt under some of the fingernails is apparent.

'This is a nice touch,' the casting director coos. She reaches forward, wanting to touch the digits – my property – BAM – my open hand slams the table and she withdraws as though she's been burned.

'Powerful,' the director says and his pen scratches down some notes on the script. 'Let it all out.'

When I pull the knife from my bag, they don't flinch. As the table tumbles over and crashes to the floor, they don't race for the door. They sit still and watch me approach, drinking me in, urging me to do my best work.

A QUIET RETRIBUTION
DAWN NICHOLSON

A little bit of pee came out when she heard the man's voice. Jan's nostrils prickled and she felt a cold draught at her back, as if someone had opened a door behind her. Turning, she pulled her shoulders back, made herself stand up straight to face the vicar, who was ushering the man towards her.

'Ladies, have you met Mr Blake?'

'Please, call me Arthur,' the man smiled. The women put aside the flowers they'd been arranging and gathered to welcome him. Jan watched the man shake hands, repeating names as the vicar introduced them all, 'Teresa, Margaret, Andrea,' still clutching her own spray of lemony carnations when he held out his hand for hers.

He'd aged, of course. His voice was deeper than she remembered but there was no doubt it was him. His hair had thinned and he'd gained weight, especially around the middle, but he still had the same slightly diffident air about him, the same easy smile he employed so winningly when she knew him, using it now to charm the ladies of the Wetherby WI.

'Arthur is interested in joining the choir,' the vicar beamed. 'I've told him, we always need more men.'

Excusing herself, Jan walked through the vestry towards the vicar's small office, aware of the mechanics of every movement, the slight, but definite, tremor at the back of her legs. She switched the computer on and stared blankly at the screen, blind to the familiar blue image, seeing instead dust motes rising in the light cast from a small corner window, deep in the past. It was him. And yet he'd looked at her blandly, with no more recognition than if she'd been a piece of furniture. When the vicar introduced her, the man had nodded, hello, hello, nice to meet you. Her face, her name, did not seem to elicit any particular flicker of remembrance. But then, why should it? Jan Hughes was a different person altogether than the Janet Phillips she'd been as a girl. But it was definitely him. Half a century on, just the sound of his voice had brought it all back: the swimming-cap smell of judo mats stacked against the wall, muffled voices from a nearby room, the tinseled wings of angels.

'Robert, love?' She says the words out loud, hoping to calm herself by invoking her late husband. Always, in moments of stress she longs to hear his voice, to be soothed by his reassuring baritone and blunt, Yorkshire vowels. Though she talks to him often, even now, he never talks back. She saw him half a dozen times the first year after he died. Putting the laundry away one afternoon, he'd startled her, sitting on the bed watching, a slow smile on his face as if she'd said something amusing. Other times she'd see him out of the corner of her eye, a figure at the top of the stairs, shifting, hazily defined. The air seemed to shimmer and she'd hold her breath, desperate to hold him there, wanting to stretch out the moment for as long as possible, to put off the time when she'd look up and he'd be gone and the house – and she along with it – would be plunged back into emptiness.

Few things give real relief from the loneliness, she's found. In the absence of a cure, she tries to keep busy. Church is good for that. She's been coming here twenty-two years now – which isn't bad for an atheist. Robert 'found Jesus' in his forties after he was caught off-guard by a couple of evangelicals in the shopping precinct. Shortly after, he started going to church, then joined the choir. At a loose end one Sunday, she'd been persuaded to go with him, curious to see if she might reignite her own, lost faith. And though she remains unconvinced of the existence of a deity, she's found she enjoys church life, reassured by its rhythms, the unchanging cycle of high days and holy days. Even the building is a comfort now, another place where Robert had been, where some part of him might remain still, embedded in the fabric of the stone walls and tapestried cushions. Nobody has ever pressed her on what she believes. Anglicans are accommodating in that way; they don't mind. So while the rest of the congregation bow their heads, she pictures summer meadows, the owl she saw on an early morning walk in Northumberland one year. Considers what to make for dinner.

Over the years, she'd taken on more responsibilities. It was easily done, what with not having children. She had more time than the other women and she liked the idea of being useful, of serving the community in some way. It started with the flowers. Then, after Robert died, she joined the WI – more for an excuse to get out of the house than anything, relieved to find herself amongst the church's jolly matriarchs, more grateful than she can say for the new friends who kept her afloat those first dark months, when everything seemed so pointless, so futile without Robert to go home to.

Theirs had been a happy marriage. Their only sadness was in remaining childless. Though they'd hoped for children, they hadn't been lucky in that way and people didn't used to make a fuss about it, not like they do nowadays. It was just one of those things. If it wasn't meant to be, you accepted it and got on with things, glad for what you did have. And she had a lot to be grateful for. Robert was a gentle man, patient. A keen gardener, he always used to bring her something from the garden when he got home from work. Even in winter he'd find something: a sprig of holly or a stem of tiny jasmine, snowdrops in the spring. In summer he'd present her with the first yellow flowers from the courgettes, delighted that first time she fried them quickly in batter and served them with honey and vinegar – the start of a new summer tradition.

She tried to maintain the garden after he died but it had been too hard in the end – not the physical work so much, but the memories. Bending to deadhead the roses, she'd break into sudden, hot tears, remembering seeing him there, his face a study in contentment as he pottered up and down, snipping and perfecting.

Now she has a young man who comes once a fortnight to do all that. The veg patch has been turfed over. Robert's shed stands locked and lonely at the bottom of the garden. She stays in the house when the young man comes. After a couple of hours, she makes him a cup of tea (white, two sugars) and takes it out to him, exchanges a few pleasantries. But she never looks at what he's done. Only after his van has pulled away does she make her way slowly down the length of the garden, lamenting that it's not a patch on how Robert kept it. There had been no courgettes again this summer. And those supermarket ones didn't taste of anything.

* * *

It was Wednesday, her afternoon to do a bit of admin for the vicar, and though it was always pleasant to do it with the choir practising in the background, today more than ever, Jan was glad of the chance to absorb herself in something for a few hours, to clear her mind of the terrible thoughts that have been plaguing her. Some of the more observant parishioners have noticed that she hasn't been her usual self these last few weeks. One or two of the WI ladies have commented on how tired she looks and even the vicar, anxious not to pry, has made quiet enquiries about the source of the trouble. Unable to confide the real cause of her disquiet, she has had to endure some well-meaning but misplaced solicitude, telling no one that in the days since Arthur Blake appeared the ground itself seems to have given way under her, that all her carefully crafted ways of being have crumbled, leaving her unprotected, exposed.

For so long, she'd been able to categorise what happened as an unpleasant period in her life, one she'd tried hard to put behind her. But now he was here it was all surfacing again, the memories sharp and clear, distressing. So far, she'd managed to avoid coming into direct contact with him, but how was she to manage it for much longer? Looking around the vicar's office at the boxes of bric-a-brac and the stack of old Bibles in need of rebinding, she feels a stab of loss. It will pain her not to come here anymore. She will miss the familiar clutter of this room with its overstuffed cushions and shabby, donated furniture, the small sense of purpose her afternoons here have given her. It will be hard to give up. And yet, that may be the only way to recover her peace of mind.

The vicar hasn't heard of data protection. A poor typist, he dictates everything from his big padded chair on the other side of the desk, reading out the minutes from the church council meeting, changing his mind over the wording of the roof appeal letter he wants to send to the handful of wealthy donors he hopes will pay for it.

'Oh, while I remember,' he says, 'can you send a welcome letter to Mr Blake for me?' He reads out the address from the back of his notebook and Jan types it into the contacts list, committing it to memory.

'Is he new to the area?' she asks.

'Yes. He's just moved into one of the bungalows on Wharton Avenue. Wanted to be nearer his son, now he's getting on a bit. Speaking of which,' he smiles, 'I've forgotten my diary again, do you mind if I nip next door and get it?'

While he's gone, Jan goes through to the church, more at ease than she's felt all week as she walks towards the choir stalls to have a quick word with Ruth Pendlebury about the Christmas fundraiser, stunned to see Arthur Blake somehow there, sitting next to the Wilson's daughter. Alice, the girl was called, all golden curls and smiles. Couldn't be more than ten. As the girl stood up to sing with the other youngsters, he did it: put his hand on the back of the child's leg and slid it briefly, but unmistakably, upwards, then removed it again just as quickly. The girl looked around, alarmed, then turned back to the choirmaster and went on singing, blinking furiously as if blinded by sudden, bright light.

It was like being catapulted back in time, as if he'd put his hand – icy cold – on the back of her own, young neck. Jan turned on her heel and rushed to the toilet, not stopping to lock the cubicle door before she threw up the egg sandwich she'd had for lunch. Staring down at the mush of soggy bread at the bottom of the bowl, she knew there was no way to unsee what she'd seen. It had happened in a moment. But it had happened.

At home later, she did something she hadn't done since the night Robert died: took his bottle of scotch and his heavy crystal glass from the living-room cabinet and poured herself three fingers of the amber liquid, gulping it down in one fiery mouthful. Pulling off her jumper, she discarded it where it fell, not bothering to fold or hang the rest of her clothes as she stumbled to the bathroom. In the shower she cried noisily, soaping every inch of her skin and hair, scrubbing herself as if she might scrub away the stain of Arthur Blake on her. By the time she emerged thirty minutes later, she was raw and pink and resolute.

She didn't sleep that night. Images from the past tormented her, things she'd thought long buried. Fifty years had passed since that man had touched her. She'd been eight when it started, just a little younger than Alice Wilson. He was eleven years her senior, an adult in every respect. He was a helper at Junior Church, not at all the stranger her parents had warned her about. And so she'd followed him willingly to the storeroom where the props were kept for the nativity, had sat down on the dusty green sports mat in the corner with no sense of foreboding, no possible way of knowing what was about to happen.

She sees now that he'd put the mat there on purpose, had planned the whole thing. Once he'd taken her into that room and done those terrible things to her, it was as if she never came out. Again and again she followed him in there, terrified he might carry out his threat and tell everyone what a dirty, filthy whore she was. Those were the words he'd used. She shudders at the memory, remembering his voice, his oily triumph every time he made her do those shameful things.

And then, as suddenly as it had started, it stopped. He seemed to just disappear. Life went back, almost, to how it had been before. Sometimes it seemed she must have imagined the whole thing. But she hadn't. He had done those things to her and the feeling of being tainted by them had never gone away. Even so, she tries to reason now, he must be over seventy, surely he couldn't... She closes her eyes, sickened to remember his hand on the back of Alice's leg, his breath as he bore down on her own small body, a great devouring monster, consuming her, making her ugly and dirty and wrong. She'd been powerless to stop him then. She would not let it happen again.

* * *

The next day passed slowly. Jan tried to fill the time with her usual activities but found herself restless, unable to settle. In the kitchen, she emptied cupboards and drawers and cleaned every surface, standing on a chair to scrub grease from the fan over the hob until the whole thing gleamed like new. After lunch she turned on the television, hoping to be calmed by her afternoon programme. Ordinarily, she enjoyed watching the contestants setting up their easels by streams and old buildings, but today she found the three amateur painters silly and talentless, the bridge they were painting unattractive. Still, she forced herself to sit through it, relieved when the credits rolled and she looked up to find the sky darkening outside, the last of the winter sunshine lighting up the row of conifers in next door's garden.

At last, by four o'clock it was dark. Jan switched on the lamps in the living room and rose to close the curtains. Outside, the wind had strengthened, rattling the letterbox and setting dogs barking in a nearby street. It would be a night for staying indoors but it was too early yet. There would be people about, on their way home from school and work. She must bide her time.

The thing about it was, she realises now, how he'd made it seem so normal. The way he ingratiated himself so completely with all the people who might have seen what was happening, so he was able to go on doing it, almost in plain sight. One time she'd seen him laughing with her mother and had stood, rooted helplessly to the spot, burning with the urge to speak, to accuse him. And then, as if he could feel her gaze through the thin cotton of his sweatshirt, he'd turned and winked at her. Looking around, she expected disapproval, puzzled frowns on the faces of the adults, but nobody reacted. It was as if none of them saw it. And she understood then that he was right, that no one would believe her.

At seven o'clock Jan pulled on her coat and buttoned it up. Put on her hat and gloves and collected her sturdy brown handbag – heavier than usual – from beside the door.

Wharton Avenue was just a ten-minute walk away and she covered the distance quickly, glad to be out of the house and moving. As she walked, she went over the plan in her head, reassured by its simplicity, gratified to notice that the single other person she passed didn't so much as glance at her. Her friend Margaret, a divorcee, was forever telling her that older women were invisible, that no one ever remembered meeting a woman over fifty. She must hope she's right.

Arriving at the house, the street was deserted. The wind, howling now, had forced people inside. She opened the gate and walked briskly up the path towards a neat, well-maintained bungalow. One half of the garden had been graveled over to make a driveway on which was parked a small, economical-looking car. Two spindly shrubs, still with labels attached, stood in pots either side of the mat.

He recognised her as soon as he opened the door.

'Mrs Hughes is it?' he said. 'What a nice surprise.' He looked over her shoulder, as if expecting her to be accompanied, frowning a little when he saw she was alone. 'Please, come in.'

Jan stepped silently over the threshold, smiling. He closed the door behind her and gestured into the living room where she could see he had the lamp on, his newspaper over the chair arm where he must have been sitting before she rang the bell. The curtains were closed.

'Now, can I offer you a cup of tea?'

* * *

By the time she left the wind had worked itself into a full-blown gale. Jan dropped the latch and closed the door quietly behind her. Looking up and down the street, she was grateful for the rain just starting to fall, the clatter of a can rolling in the gutter. Not a soul was about. All along the street, she imagined people sitting in the yellow lit rooms, getting on peacefully with their lives. She pictured them eating dinner, watching television, putting their children to bed. It would be better for all of them now. She clicked the gate shut and stepped smartly down the road.

It was Tuesday before anyone found him. His son had been calling all day, and when he still hadn't answered by nine o'clock, had gone round and found him. *Bludgeoned* was the headline in the local paper. She'd considered messing the place up, making it look like a burglary, but decided against it because she wanted people to ask why this had happened, what could this quiet, unassuming man have done to warrant so savage an attack? Fifty years separated the day he took her into the props room and the day he put his hand on the back of Alice Wilson's leg. She cannot believe he's led a blameless life all that time. There will people who know the answer to her question. There will, surely, be others.

She has thought about what would happen if she were caught, sent to jail. The idea isn't so terrifying as it might once have been. She's old enough to think she might be of some use to the young women in there, though she'd miss her mattress. She has a very good mattress on her bed now, extra firm. Robert preferred something softer, but now that she sleeps alone, she's invested in a hard, unyielding mattress and her back doesn't ache nearly so much in the morning as it used to.

* * *

Over two thousand sexual images of children were uncovered when police searched Arthur Blake's bungalow. Local people remembered seeing him outside a playground several times in the weeks before his death. These are not small things. The thing she did is not a small thing.

* * *

Lately the papers are full of reports of *sexual predators*: men who are alleged to have assaulted many women over many decades. Women who kept quiet. She's not sure how she feels about this fashion for telling so long after the fact, not sure it's worth raking up the past only to be torn to shreds by lawyers, to have your words twisted, reputation destroyed. But then she thinks of Alice Wilson's startled expression, the way her own bladder unclenched at the sound of Arthur Blake's voice, the fear and shame that engulfed her, even after all this time. Set against what he'd done and might have gone on to do, her act of retribution seems reasonable, proportionate. She may sleep soundly on her tightly sprung mattress.

She does.

THE ENDS
ANDREW HUDSON

I get all the little Crooks in the minibus and off we go. It holds seventeen, including me, but both passenger seats up front are vacant. Even though the only other lasses on this little excursion are going by car, a car too small to squeeze in yet another pair of white high heels and a miniskirt, Shell would rather be in the back with just one more empty seat between her and twelve hormone-sweating lads than sat with me. She has nothing to say to any of them, of course; head down, thumbs tapping away on her Nokia, sending a scathing report on her company to someone in that car, no doubt.

For their part, the lads had just enough sense to steal a glance at her legs as they were climbing in and nothing more. They know I can see everything in the rear-view mirror, and they def don't want me pissed off before the party's even begun. So instead it was a chain of mostly broken voices saying *Alreet, Bry* as they trooped on, the bravest of them attempting an *Alreet, Shell* and being ignored, and then the hour's drive from Crook to the disco being held by the Young Farmers' Club at Vale of Eden is filled with loud talk and laughing, and the occasional hush as someone sneaks a swig of something behind the headrests and they all wait to see if I'll notice.

As if I could care less. I'm no one's dad, just the driver. Though if that bottle ends up in Shell's hands there'll be fucking hell to pay, but anyway it doesn't.

We crunch over the rough gravel of the car park and I pull up right outside what's basically a jumbo portacabin with a peaked roof by Ikea, about as thrilling as you'd expect for a village cricket and football club built in the sixties on the edge of the Pennines. None of Crook Memorial Hall's stone-and-slate style – though you'd be hard pressed to fit in just my passengers back there, let alone all the late-teen members of Lancashire's various YFCs at once. This place has everything that's needed for that, though, which is to say a big main room and a bar licence.

Not necessarily everything that's wanted, mind.

Shell is first out ('Well this is the absolute ends,' she mutters, which must have come as a shock since that's what she says about Crook usually), cautiously hobbling towards the little red two-door her mates are popping out of and trying not to break a heel or an ankle on the way. Then the lads jump down one by one, clustering at the clubhouse entrance, peering through the windows to see how many are already inside.

I get out myself to make sure the minibus's sliding side door is closed and locked properly. My last passenger off has a ciggie on his lip already. 'Got a light, Bry?' he asks, and I roll my eyes. But I spark it up for him.

'You waiting around then?' he asks next.

'Yes, Thomas. Me and the minibus you'll be riding home in too.'

'Oh reet. Aye, the bus.' He clears his throat and drags on his ciggie.

'I'll be parked just over there,' I tell him, and point to a spot at the edge of the gravel, about halfway between the clubhouse and a tall floodlight that hits the playing field and illuminates that half of the car park too. I wouldn't much want to be right underneath that, but nearby isn't a bad idea. The best shadows are near the light.

'Oh reet.' He gives me a significant look. I roll my eyes again and he grins. 'We'll be careful what we say, like, don't fret.'

'See that you are,' I tell him. 'Now, why don't you get this lot inside, you'd think they were scared of girls or being seen dancing or sumat.'

I slam shut the sliding door and climb back in to park up, trundling past Shell and her little posse stiltwalking the other way. Shell ignores me, but a few of the lasses giggle and wave and I give them a smile and a little wave back. By the time I've three-pointed the minibus and locked up, the lot of them are inside.

I study the car park for a moment – it's the staff's cars probably that are lined up nearest the bins and the back entrance, plus a few others dotted about here and there – and then I try to give the clubhouse the benefit of the doubt. Nope: it's fugly and then some. The absolute ends... *of the earth*, as Shell too-coolly always leaves unsaid.

I squint out at the playing field, the dark rise of the Pennines beyond, the clear sky turning to evening. It was a nice day, today.

Hopefully it'll be a good night.

* * *

Inside is simultaneously dim and saturated with vivid light. Depending where and when you look everyone is painted over green or red or blue, leaning towards each other to shout over the Britpop. There's probably forty or so including my lot, single-sex groups around the tall tables about the walls, handling their plastic pints of lager and bottles of whatever rainbow-tinted alcopop shite the lasses are drinking. All the staff are behind the bar, because there's not been time to make enough mess to go clean up, and the big space cleared in the centre for a dance floor is deserted, because no one's had time to drink enough to be the first out on it.

That'll be Shell and her mates, probably. Some gang of lasses, at least; there look to be a few more threes and fours here. Certainly it'll be none of the Crook lads, not unless 'Tubthumping' comes on early, in which case they'll form a scrum and be jumping up and down in no time.

I head for the bar and catch the eye of one of the maids, maybe in her mid-twenties and short enough she wouldn't be able to see over my shoulder.

'What'll it be?' she asks.

'Just a Coke, please, love.' She raises her eyebrows, and a flicker of defensiveness is provoked. 'I'll be driving some of this lot back down Kendall way later on.'

'Not for about five hours.' She fishes the pop-hose from its holster and smiles as she squirt-guns Coke into a glass with ice in it. 'Could pop some Jack Daniels in this for you.'

I shake my head and smile back. 'Proper whisky'd be better. But best not. Besides, I've been to a few of these older YF dos in the past. You never know when a couple of strapping lads need a more strapping lad to step in and calm things down.'

'Chaperone duty, eh?' She sets my drink on the bar. 'You look like you could carry one or two under your arm.'

'And I have.'

'One-twenty-five, please.'

I pass her a fiver. 'Any food tonight?'

'Kitchen'll microwave pizzas, pasties and chips until ten. And we have crisps and the usual at the bar.'

'Okay, maybe later. Thanks.'

I collect my change, sip my Coke, and survey the room. It'd be a lie to say that every lad in here had a working farmer's build, but more than a few must spend their weekends stacking hay in the barn beside their fathers, and probably would keep on doing so instead of going to college. Or as well as going, I suppose, since that's what I did. For a while, anyway.

Blur starts playing, that 'Boys and Girls' crap, and if that wasn't enough reason to go somewhere else the doors open and a bunch more young farmers and their sisters arrive from some other nearby club, a couple of taxis turning around in the car park behind them. And since the bar will be their first stop, I'm taking my Coke and going back to the minibus for a bit, because it has a CD player, and someone thought to bring along a couple of flexible twenty-disc carry packs, didn't he? And enough CDs of actually decent music to fill one of them too.

I glance back as I push through the door. Shell is on the dance floor, arms draped in the air as she steps and sways, one of her friends joining her as all those strapping lads look on.

* * *

In the gaps between the songs that I like, I can make out the muffled seconds of whatever is playing in the clubhouse. At one point I recognise the morse code stutter of the keyboard on 'Sorted for E's and Wizz', and that feels like a sign when I see Thomas and a couple of youths I don't recognise emerge, hunching around the lighter he obviously had on him earlier to fire up their ciggies. Thomas looks my way, then they wander over to the minibus.

'Alreet, Bry,' he says, keeping his voice nice and comfortably low, and no need for an excuse this time either.

'Thomas,' I reply. 'Alright, lads,' I say to the others.

'Thomas says you can help us out,' one of them says by greeting.

'Does he? Well, I might have a little something on me for myself that I could part with. What did you have in mind?'

'Weed and speed,' Thomas whispers, and giggles.

'One or the other, I'd have thought.'

'These two want to smoke,' he continues. 'But me and a few of the lads—'

'No need for the whole story,' I say. The conversation has been conducted through the driver's-side window, me up in the seat with the dregs of my Coke balanced on the dash, them standing in the dusk outside. Out of sight of prying eyes, I flip one of the CD carriers on the seat beside me to the 'empty' back pockets and slip out a couple of baggies: one contains a row of single-paper joints, the other a scatter of little folded paper squares.

A few notes change hands, as do two joints and two wraps.

'Don't smoke those near the bins unless you want the staff to know what you're doing,' I tell them. 'I'd go round the other side from the main doors. Further from the road, too. You tried it before?'

'Of course,' says one of them.

'Of course,' I say back. 'Maybe save one for later anyway, eh? It's good stuff.'

'Alreet, thanks,' says the other.

'Thanks, Bry,' says Thomas.

'Careful who sees that, eh?' I tell him, and he gives me the thumbs up as they head back to the bad music.

Good stuff, I claim. Alright stuff, maybe, but it smells the part. And young blood will take to a lightly loaded joint just fine. If they come back for more, well, they can buy from the stronger bag next time.

I drain my Coke, then roll up the window and step down, lock the minibus and head back inside. There's been a steady flow of drop-offs the last half hour and there are enough bodies drinking now that they're encroaching on the dance floor. Some are even dancing.

Thomas is receiving slaps on the back; there's a huddle, then he heads off to the toilets. It's only as I'm ordering another Coke and a mini pizza that one of his mates leaves the group and heads after him – good lad, Thomas, not stupid, not drawing attention. They take it in turns, one disappearing off, another returning, never more than three of them in there at once.

My ham, cheese and pineapple dinner comes out of the kitchen hot and soft on a paper dish. As I take it and my Coke and myself outside, Thomas and company are finally taking to the floor, hooting and cheering at themselves, dancing with all the grace but at least also the enthusiasm of bouncy newborn lambs.

'Oh, *pizza,*' says one of my two customers, as they stumble around from the dark side of the building and find me and my treasures spotlit by the lamp over the entrance. The other starts sniggering in a way that probably won't stop for a while.

Bless.

* * *

Word quietly gets around. *No Smoking* in the clubhouse means there's always a legit reason for people to nip outside for five or ten minutes; and if they happen to wander into the vicinity of my minibus, well, there's nothing wrong with that, is there? A few from Shell's little gaggle of girlfriends buy wraps, though I know Shell won't partake, she doesn't touch any of this stuff. An hour later I brave the disco to find the gents and offload some of that Coke I've been guzzling, and at the urinals a tubby lad masking barnyard BO with Old Spice asks if I've got any E. 'Not on me' is the answer, but ten minutes later I've sold him six half-pills.

In a quiet spell after midnight I get out and lean against the wall between gravel and grass. The floodlight onto the playing field is off, so it just gets the backwash from the smaller one shining on the car park; but that one's behind me and on the other side of the bus, so my night vision isn't ruined. The stars are out, and with next to no light pollution the uplands lie darker than the sky, a deep near-black the eye wants filled with detail that isn't there.

I hear the kitchen door of the clubhouse open; the plastic bump and bang of a big bin lid; then grinding footsteps on the loose stone coming my way. It's the little barmaid.

'Hello,' I say.

She leans against the wall too, close, arms folded. My elbows are down on the top of it; the same height comes up to her shoulders. 'I had you pegged as the responsible one, didn't I?' she says.

'Supremely safe driver, me, I assure you.'

'You know what I mean,' she scoffs. 'Taking a bit of a risk, don't you think? You can hardly make a fast getaway in that thing, even if you don't wait to pick up all the customers you brought with.'

I laugh a little, feeling around for my ciggies. 'It's not going to come to that.'

'Better hope not. We do have cops north of Kendall. If eighty baby farmers get fucked up and start causing trouble, someone'll be sent out. Cumbria Police HQ is in Penrith, you know, that's just round the corner.'

'If anything causes trouble, it'll be the beer. Or those horrible drinks like strawberry pop with vodka hidden in it.' I pause to light up. 'Look. They're not kids, just lads and lasses having some fun before adulthood and the year two thousand hits them. And nothing they get from me is going to give them a bad time. A few mild joints. A bit of speed with icing sugar ground in so the dabs taste sweet. They'll dance it off smiling and nobody will ever know the difference.'

She reaches out and pinches my cig. 'Friendly neighbourhood tambourine man, eh?' The cherry end glows, her face lit in gentle amber, then she blows out a plume of smoke and doesn't hand it back.

I shrug. 'I know all them I brought here, and I know the rest are basically the same. They're going to go after whatever they want, and someone always shows up to this kind of thing with some kind of dope. Honestly? I'm surprised one of you lot isn't selling.' I hold a hand out for my cig, then hesitate dramatically. 'Oh, is that what this is? You're warning me off your turf?'

She giggles. 'You cheeky bastard.' She takes another drag then hands it back over. 'Actually, I was sort of wondering what that speed is like.'

I raise my eyebrows. 'This conversation's certainly changeable.'

She grins in the darkness. 'What can I say. It's a long night, and the music in there's hardly my cup of tea. Some of it anyway.'

'I know what you mean. Alright, come on then. I'm Bryan, by the way.'

'Wendy. So, Bryan, what can I get for a pint of Coke and a bag of pork scratchings?'

* * *

I give Wendy a good deal, though not quite as good as that, and late as it is I do tax a dab out of her wrap to wake myself up a little. One of my sugar-free grown-up mixes, but I only charge her the junior mix rate. I still want that comped Coke, of course, and I'm all set to follow her in the back way until she points me at the proper entrance and sends me packing. We reconnect on opposite sides of the bar and I blag a packet of salt-and-vinegar too. The other staff soon have a pep in their step if I'm one to judge.

It has indeed been a pretty reasonable night, and now it's winding up. There's a decent fold of notes in my pocket, and as I survey the disco all I see are happy-looking people, some slow-dancing to the relentlessly shit music of these late nineties, others chatting or watching from the sidelines. Testimony to how good my speed is that even my foot starts tapping to 'Why Does It Always Rain On Me?', the worst sound to come out of Scotland since the bagpipes.

It takes me half my Coke and all the crisps to click that Shell is nowhere to be seen. After that it's the work of a minute or two to spot her friends dancing their little hearts out, none of them absent and paired off with her in the loos.

No. Fucking not a chance. Not at a fucking Young Farmers disco. Not with some shit-kicking, sheep-shagging, animal husbandry byproduct side-of-beef dickhead moron.

Just, no.

The main door bangs off the wall and slams shut behind me and I'm back outside. A quick stalk around the car park and there's no cars fogged up or rocking; I loop around by the minibus, the bins, the back entrance – nothing; and then, because the thing you lost is always in the last place you look, I check the far corner of the clubhouse and stop dead.

Shell, with her arms loose around the neck of some scrawny bod not even her height out of heels, which are dangling by their straps from her fingers. He's wearing tan slacks and a black T-shirt, the kind with a collar and no list of gigs on the back, and his hands are way down low behind her back, and damned if her miniskirt doesn't look mini-er than earlier.

'Oi! Stop that right now, you cunt.'

Shell screams a little through mushed-up lips, her eyes staring wide at me over the little fucker's ear. Then she recognises me and pushes him back so she can shout, 'Bry! Oh, go fuck off, will you?'

'I don't think so,' I tell her, and take a good look at the cheeky shit trying it on. He's not got the YF vibe at all, probably someone's guest invite, probably never set foot on a farm since he was in primary school, probably not even from the north. Not even wearing fucking jeans.

'I'm not having that,' says this guy wearing Shell's lipgloss. 'Apologise.'

'Like fuck I will.'

Have to give him credit, he actually squares up to me, though he almost has to crane his neck to do it. 'I don't care who she is to you,' he says, 'give her an apology now, or I'll knock one out of you.'

I stare at him like he's from another planet. 'It's you I'm calling the cunt, lad.'

'Oh.' He still looks less than pleased about that, as you'd expect. 'You can apologise direct to me, then.'

I snort, because he's got balls to even ask. But also, I can't help but notice that this little scrap was about to defend Shell's honour of all things, and against a pissed-off bastard like myself twice his size. Maybe I do owe him an apology.

'That,' I say, 'is my sister.'

'Oh,' he says again. He groans and shakes his head. 'Fucking Young Farmers,' he mutters. 'Everyone's always some big bugger's sister.'

'Some big fucking arsehole's sister,' Shell spits at me. 'You don't own me, Bryan, and you don't get a say in what I do, so piss off.'

'Look,' I say, feeling a bit foolish actually, 'maybe I… what's your name?'

'Martin.' He's still standing half between me and Shell, but his guard is coming down a bit. The tension dissipating.

'And who are you?'

Shell gives me a painfully bright smile that doesn't reach her eyes. 'He's the one I'm going to be snogging again,' she says, 'as soon as you,' she adds, 'piss off!' she shouts.

'Maybe you had better, you know, just piss off?' suggests this Martin.

He's trying not to laugh.

Suddenly so am I.

'Alright,' I manage, 'I'll piss off. Martin, I'm sorry. Shell, I'm sorry that you left it this late, you've got about half an hour before the minibus leaves.'

'Oh, I'll be just fine,' she says, 'don't wait for me.'

'Whoa.' I'm not about to laugh now. 'You're getting on that bus and that's all.'

'Fuck off, Bry.'

'I'm not leaving you in the fucking ends at one in the morning.'

'I've got a car,' says Martin.

'That's nice,' I tell him, 'she is not getting in it.'

'Bry, will you please fuck off?'

'I came here with two mates,' he says. 'I'm the designated driver. I've not touched a drop all night.'

'I don't care if you never drank in your life,' I tell him, but for god's sake, could this little bastard please say something unreasonable, just once?

He turns to Shell. 'They live ten minutes from here. I can drop them off and give you a lift. Where do you live?'

'Crook.'

'Near Kendall? That's a nice drive, no problem.'

'It's an hour each way,' I say.

He shrugs. 'Good company for half that, though.'

'You are really sweet,' Shell tells him, 'let's go and talk about it. Somewhere else,' she adds, nailing me with the evil eye, and then she backs away and pulls him with her, into the darkness of the clubhouse side where the stoners go when I send them that way, and the last thing I see of them is Martin giving me that face over his shoulder, the face that means *what did you expect* or *this is out of our hands* or... fuck it, I don't know.

Something.

They're gone.

Leaving me here with nothing but the distant sound of breaking glass.

* * *

Nothing moves in the car park.

I stare at it, all of it, without focus, for several seconds, but... nothing.

I glance away to where Shell and Martin aren't, or can't be seen at least, then start back along the front of the clubhouse, the only sounds the thump and throb of the music inside and the clicking and grinding under my soles. The sharp close brightnesses from the light over the entrance and coming down from that high floodlight ruin my night vision, turning the parked cars into gleaming slabs of cold colour, dark voids framed behind their windshields and windows; the expanse of gravel is an endless irregular chessboard of washed out grey on black, the crushed stones and their tiny shadows forming countless shapes and patterns instead of ordered squares and lines.

I pass the entrance, and with its light behind me I get sight more back. And I start to run, because now I can see the one thing about the minibus that differs from all the other vehicles parked here.

Its cabin light is on.

I skid around the bonnet, scattering gravel. Not the one thing: the driver's-side door is open, the window put right through so someone could pull the lock. There's chunks of safety glass on the dashboard, in the footwell, and scattered all over the driver's seat – except for a rough oblong where my CD carriers used to be but aren't.

'Fuck,' I say, with a calm that I really don't feel. 'Fucking arsehole!' I shout, which feels a lot more on point. Then the calm hits after all, carried by the thought that there weren't more than a couple of seconds between me hearing the glass break and me not seeing anyone in the car park.

Right behind the minibus, I reckon.

No way for me to sneak over on gravel.

Fuck it.

I fish the keys from my pocket, stick them in the ignition, and twist. The engine turns over with a rumble, all the parking lights come on, and I jab the fog lights too for good measure. Behind the minibus everything is suddenly bathed in heavy, evil red.

'If you leave my shit behind and start running, I won't chase you,' I tell the night, and I don't hear anything so I just stride down the length of the bus anyway, going wide as I come around the back, fists bunched, and there's fucking no one there, god damn it. Just a pink cloud of exhaust fumes drifting through the crimson glow.

I look about and immediately notice a brick-sized chunk is missing from the top of the old wall I was leaning on before: just the thing for smashing a window. And then, beyond it, in the darkness where the playing field used to be, something moves, a rusty ghost fading the further it gets from the infernal haze of my foglights. And I don't see my CD carriers left behind, and I don't know if whoever it is has their pockets stuffed with my gear or not, no way to tell with them off in the dark, is there? So I do chase them, I run to the wall and plant both hands, plant a foot to vault over and chase that bastard down, except then something jumps up into the light, a red smear on the black, fast and close, like a big lump of stone with five fingertips around it, and I—

—hear the crunch of gravel—

—like my forehead is the car park under my feet, and all the stars swim, and I hear the crunch of gravel again but from right behind my head now, and the stars go still, all the stars, oh but no, now they're turning, turning and turning, only not so bright anymore, not as bright at these big red stars, so close, two stars, I think they are. Blinding. I should close my eyes. Although they're fading too.

I can't hear shit music, that's a relief. Can't hear anything. Wonder what that barmaid is doing now the disco is over.

Shell has a ride back home, I remember, which is good.

Because she thinks this place is the ends.

THAT CRUCIBLE SUMMER
PETE HARDY

Sunday, 20 November 2022. There are seven of us. We're walking across Burbage Moor, a handful of miles outside Sheffield. I've had some desperate days tramping around the Peak District in autumn, but today is the worst, because we're going to the place where Ben Davy was finally found.

The peaty trail skirts boggy hollows and threads through a chaos of boulders. The tall, proud grasses of summer are dying back, faded, bent, and soaked by a stubbornly wet November. Mist hangs about our hunched shoulders, held motionless in the valley as if cupped in supplicating hands.

The path rises and dips until we join the rough, car-wide track that runs to the valley head a mile away. DI Stuart Bingham, shaven-headed, stocky build, his face seasoned by service, opens a metal five-bar gate and we pass through with stones skittering and crunching under our feet. As we follow the track we take halting, uneven strides to avoid ruts and ankle-deep puddles. A hidden red grouse cackles in protest as we invade its territory.

At the top of an incline we come to a tired bench that bears a dulled brass commemorative plaque. *In Loving Memory Of D.J.R. 1947 – 1998. She Loved This View.* No roads in sight now. The land feels hidden, secretive. The press have agreed to stay away, though we know they are waiting for us back at Fox House Inn, pacing about the car park like a keening hound pack, getting ready.

The detective leading the way, DCI Frank Niven, halts, and looks at Kath, Ben's sister. His hazel eyes are thoughtful, sharply intent on pursuing his work. Grey is showing in his hair at the temples. His blue Barbour coat was probably a recent purchase specially for today. 'I'll wait with DI Bingham while you lay your flowers,' he says. 'Take as long as you need.'

'Is it… here? Where?' Kath asks, seeming uncertain, more fragile.

'This way, lovey,' DC Sonia Lister, the Family Liaison Officer, says. Her accent has a Midlands ring to it, and I guess she comes from Coventry or Leicester. She might be fifteen years younger than her colleagues. She's slim, looks like she might be a keen runner. Her short, spiky fair hair is shaved closer at the nape of her neck. Her tan leather jacket shows some wear at the elbows. On her left wrist she has a Sheffield Pride bracelet. 'Mind how you go my darling, it gets a bit slippery.' She moves off the track and follows a sinew of foot-flattened grass that heads down towards a rushing brook.

We tread with heightened care, our legs stroked by coppered bracken, as we progress through a boulder field until we come to a flat-topped outcrop of gritstone speckled with scabs of lichen. DC Lister steps around the rock, stands at the lowest side and, with an open hand, indicates a patch of ground that has recently been disturbed and carefully relaid. A shiny knot of police tape flicks and twitches in a skeletal clump of dead heather behind her.

'Here, Kath. This is where your brother was found. I'm so sorry my love.'

I take hold of Kath's arm and feel her shaking. Her gloved hands are gripping a bunch of tight-budded supermarket carnations. She's aged since I saw her in March at her father's funeral, and could now pass for ten years older than me instead of five. She's lost so much weight that she seems brittle, like her bones are made of glass. She glances at the dark soil and settling sods of grass, squeezes her eyes shut, crow's-feet deepening, and her tears finally come.

DC Lister moves away, allowing the three of us to gather closer to Kath. I hear Dan sniffing next to me, he rubs at his nose with a knuckle. Ross sighs as if in pain, takes his Calvin Klein glasses off, and runs a hand down over his face. I take a deep breath, straighten my spine, fight stinging eyes and a sudden shocking urge to throw up.

Kath places the flowers at the foot of the rock, blows a kiss, and begins to speak, head bowed. Her breath bubbles in the skin-numbing air.

'Our Father... who art in heaven... hallowed... hallowed be thy name.' Every syllable of the prayer seems to carry the agony she's been holding in for the last forty-six years. She gasps, 'Amen.' Lister, Dan, Ross and I repeat the small word and it seems to grow, then drift away, filling the valley with our grief.

I raise my head, wipe a tear from my stubbly jawline. Above us I can see Niven and Bingham. They're motionless, observing us, fisted hands sunk in their coat pockets. Beyond them I can just make out the beginning of the climbers' route rising to the fractured wall of Burbage Rocks, now wider and more eroded than when I was young.

And a memory creeps forward, like a weasel approaching a nest of cooling, untended grouse eggs. I remember a spot high up on the rocks where I sat with Dad one time. He'd followed the deadly progress of a hunting kestrel through his ancient binoculars, while I'd studied the heavily creased OS map until I was bored and fidgety.

We'd been so close to this terrible place. So close.

It was achingly hot that day when I followed Dad along foot-burning trails, our blood boiling, skin reddening, flying ants pestering. As hot as the day they took Ben in that crucible hot summer of seventy-six.

* * *

It was too warm to play football in the street by ten, so we sat at the roadside in the shade cast by a tired looking maple. Melting tar glistened at the kerb edges and stuck to the soles of our cheap trainers. Even in the shade the tar bled from between the gravel.

The four of us watched as a ladybird became trapped on a two-pence-coin-sized sticky spot. It fluttered its wings for a few minutes, then was still. We agreed its death wasn't a huge tragedy because, after all, there were plenty of ladybirds that summer when we learned the meaning of 'drought'.

For us drought meant lining up at a standpipe in the street each morning with a couple of buckets or large cooking pans to fill. Drought meant remembering not to pour any of the precious water down the toilet when we'd had a pee. And drought meant no baths, so we became used to having strip washes with a damp, soapy flannel at the bathroom sink. Not having a bath didn't seem a great problem to me or any other lads. The four of us were eleven, and looking forward to starting at the comprehensive in September with rising levels of dread.

The streets were quiet. Everyone else on the estate was indoors where it was slightly cooler, but just as airless and exhausting. The day was unfolding in its predictable way. At half past four the men working the morning shift went off to the steel works, barely a mile away. The ones who did the night shift and finished at five were now struggling to sleep on sheetless beds. Those on afternoons and due to start work at one were already thinking about getting up.

'I had six slices o' toast for brekky,' Dan said, rubbing a hand over his belly. He lay back on the pavement, closed his eyes, and smiled.

'What's your record?' Ross said, pushing his brown-framed NHS glasses up his peeling nose.

'Nine,' said Dan.

Ben grunted like a pig and elbowed me in the ribs.

'Pillock,' I shouted and tried to give him a dead-leg but didn't hit him hard enough.

'I could scoff a screwball,' Dan said.

'I wish I could jump into a giant one,' I said, wiping my face with my *Starsky and Hutch* T-shirt.

Ross said, 'I wish I could swim in the sea and…'

'Get eaten by a shark, like that one in *Jaws*!' Ben yelled.

'Knob head,' Ross said.

I threw a stone across the street. It landed at the foot of the high wall in front of the vicarage. 'This is crap. I'll be glad when we're back at school. I've got my uniform. I can do a right good knot in my tie.'

'Loser Lorton, you are so bleedin' sad. School holidays and you're practising doing your fuckin' tie,' Ben said and flicked the top of my left ear. He knew I hated it when he did that. I got up, walked away from him and sat next to Dan.

A van chug-chugged up the hill, slowed to a crawl as it went by, and soon stopped. It was off-white, with jagged lines of rust creeping along the rims of the wheel arches. Dark fumes sputtered from the rattling exhaust pipe. After a few seconds the engine grumbled, gears clattered, the van reversed and stopped in front of us.

The window of the dented passenger door was grimy and open an inch or so. We could hear Abba on the radio. The window was lowered, streaked glass screeching. A woman leaned out. There was a man behind her in the driving seat, his eyes hidden behind mirrored sunglasses. The woman's blonde hair was tied in a messy ponytail, mascara smudged on her eyelids. She winked and took a drag from a cigarette. 'Fancy earnin' a few bob for an hour o' graft?'

I knew she wasn't a local by her accent. I thought she was Irish, or Scottish, but wasn't sure.

The four of us looked at each other and shrugged uncertainly.

'See, we need some leaflets droppin'. We're collecting owd clothes and the like. Be a nice easy job for strappin' young men like yourselves.' She showed us a rolled-up plastic bag that had a leaflet attached to it with a green rubber band. 'A few hundred o' these. Take no time at all.'

Ben pushed his curly, black hair away from his eyes. 'How much will you give us?'

'A crisp pound note.'

'Each?' Ben asked. It was more of a demand than a question. He had a confident way of talking to grown-ups that I tried to copy but never managed to carry it off like he could. Cocky, but not arrogant. Cheeky, not insolent.

'Aye, go on then. A pound each.'

Ben looked at us. 'Sounds alright, don't it?'

We nodded, following his lead as usual, stood, and rubbed the seats of our jeans down.

The woman got out of the van. Her denim skirt was short and seemed tight across her rounded belly. She had red flip-flops on her feet. She opened the rear doors, jerked a thumb. 'Hop in. We'll drop you off here when you're done.'

We clambered into the van and she closed the doors.

The van stank of oil and cigarettes. At the back was a metal chest with the lid secured by a large padlock. There were coiled lengths of thin, blue rope and what looked like a folded-up sleeping bag on top of the chest. The floor was covered with a grubby sheet, tacky against my hands. Greyed sunlight came through two cracked panes of glass at the top of the doors. The four of us glanced at each another, wordlessly wondering why we'd decided to get in. A lump came in my throat, and I was hoping Mum and Dad wouldn't hear about this.

Ross scratched at his short, ginger hair.

Dan tugged at his Leeds United shirt. It was a couple of sizes too big for him, a hand-me-down from Finn, his older brother.

Ben sat on one of the wheel arches, rubbing his hands together. 'A fuckin' quid, just for sticking bags through doors. Good, eh?'

The van jerked forward, did a noisy three-point turn, and was driven down the hill. I could tell we were turning onto the old estate of terraced houses. Our arses were bouncing, and our backs thudding against the side panels. We could hear the muffled, raised voices of the woman and the man.

The van braked hard and the woman pulled the doors open. We tumbled out, and again wiped down the seats of our jeans. Before our eyes adjusted to the sunlight, she forced bundles of bags and leaflets into our clumsy hands.

'Right my lovelies. Two of you each side o' the street. One leaflet and bag through every door. We'll meet you at the corner. Run now!' She suddenly seemed less friendly, and was biting at a ragged thumb nail. Standing close to her I noticed a faded bruise below her left eye.

We ran at first, but soon slowed to a fast-paced walk. I paired up with Ben. As always, he wanted to be competitive and kept elbowing me out of his way. We pushed leaflets and bags through letter flaps that were halfway up some doors, or at the bottom of others. The woman shouted, telling us to hurry up. At every corner she forced more bundles into our hands, and the van moved ahead again. I couldn't catch a clear sight of the man's face. He seemed heavy framed, with long, uncombed hair. Every now and then he swore at the woman.

We carried on for more than an hour and I lost track of which streets we'd been up or down. I was sweaty, hot-footed, and annoyed by the crunchy dog shit that the soles of my trainers were flattening on the dusty pavements.

Then, finally, we'd left the terraces behind, only the four short streets of semis with their garages, driveways and grassed front gardens to do. Every lawn was the colour of straw.

As I went round a corner there was a push on my back. I stumbled, sprawled on the pavement, scraping the skin off the heel of my right hand. I pressed my stinging hand against my shirt, forced back tears, looked up. Ben laughed at me.

'Bastard fucker!' I shouted. He crossed his eyes, stuck his tongue out and laughed again.

He was like that sometimes. You'd be having a good time and he'd do something to wind you up, something that made you pissed off at him, but not to the point where you'd start scrapping. And he always laughed it off. Always got away with it somehow. He was supposed to be my best mate, but sometimes he wasn't.

I told him to fuck off. He rubbed his eyes in a mock cry, then carried on.

We dropped the last of the leaflets off in a quiet cul-de-sac and the woman barked, 'Get in the van!' Minutes later we stood on the pavement in front of the vicarage. She gave us our money. The pound notes were dirty and torn. I inspected mine and worried it might be fake.

The woman said, 'Cheers lads,' opened the passenger door, but before she climbed in the man said something to her, and she hesitated, turned to us, took a drag and flicked the tab end of her fag in the gutter. 'Need a lift home?'

Three of us shook our heads. Dan and Ross began running in the direction of the chippy.

Ben looked at his Casio watch. 'Are you going past the library, by the roundabout?'

'Aye. We're headin' down there to get on the motorway,' the woman said, lighting another fag. 'Hop in the back my lovely. We'll drop you off.'

Ben told me he was supposed to be meeting his mum in ten minutes. 'I've got to go. See you tomorrow Mikey. Same time,' he said, grinning and waving his tattered pound note in the air like he was rich.

'If I can be bothered,' I said, sticking two fingers up at him. His crazy grin grew wider. I almost smiled back at him but stopped myself.

The woman closed the van doors behind Ben and climbed in the front. She blew a ring of smoke through the open window, turned the radio up, and waved. As the van went I heard Thin Lizzy telling me the boys were back in town.

My hand ached. Blood had dried on my shirt. I was glad Ben had gone. I hated him.

I can still see the pound note in Ben's hand flicking back and forth, his hair plastered with sweat to his head, the sunburnt reddening of his face, the chipped tooth that he got when we were sword fighting with broom handles, and I know I could have stopped him getting in the van again. But I hadn't.

It wasn't until later, when his dad came hurrying to our house after tea, that I thought something bad had happened. I heard him at the back door, talking in a rush, saying to Mum, 'Has your Michael seen Ben? Does he know where he is?'

Then my insides knotted, my legs felt like they were melting, and I knew it was my fault.

* * *

Kath tells us she'd like some time on her own. 'You understand, don't you? I need to talk to him,' she says, looking sadder than anyone I've ever seen.

The four of us go up to the track where Niven and Bingham are waiting. The mist above our heads seems to glow as the sun begins to burn through.

Sonia Lister joins Niven and Bingham and they talk together in hushed tones.

I glance at Ross and Dan. They're lost in their own thoughts, give me half-hearted smiles, shoot nervous looks at the detectives. I only see them three or four times a year. Sometimes I drive down from Cumbria to visit Dad at the care home and don't let them know I'm in town. When we meet up it seems there's a dark void between us where Ben should be, and we tiptoe around mentioning him until we can't bear it any longer. Then we tell the stories we've been going over and embellishing for years, the ones that make us smile, the ones that give us belly laughs until we have tears in our eyes. But today the tears are stinging, and trying to hold them back is agonising.

Hardest of all is going to see Kath, always close to her birthday and Christmas. She still lives in the family home, a dozen doors from our old house. She's on her own now, seems to find comfort from the clutter of dusty knick-knacks and framed family photos taken at Blackpool and Scarborough. When I sit on the sofa Ben looks at me from a couple of school photos on the mantlepiece, and I always hear his voice a little louder, clearer.

'*I've got to go. See you tomorrow Mikey. Same time.*'

Kath is talking quietly, hands clasped together. After a couple of minutes she blows another kiss to the cold earth, and comes up to us. Dan hugs her and the two of them walk away arm in arm. She dabs a handkerchief at her puffy eyes, and seems to have shrunk down into her crimson, quilted Primark coat.

DI Bingham opens the gate again, holds it until we've filed through, closes it with a loud clang. He stands as solidly as a sack of Orgreave coal.

DCI Niven faces us. There's something in the way he surveys people around him that quietly announces he's in charge. 'I know today must be difficult for you all, especially you Kath.'

Sonia Lister cups a hand under Kath's elbow. 'You're doing really well love. I can take you home soon.'

'Thank you, Sonia,' Kath says, her voice cracking.

Niven rocks on his heels, frowns before speaking. 'Now, we need to deal with the press. It'll only take a few minutes, but it's essential.' His accent is local, working-class roots, straight to the point. 'I'll read a statement, and I'd ask you to stand together behind me. DC Lister will speak on behalf of Kath. I'll invite questions. There's no need for you to say anything, if you don't want to.' He pauses, looks at me, Ross and Dan.

'That's a relief,' Dan mutters. His face is flushed with colour and he looks like he used to at school whenever the rare prospect of standing on the stage during morning assembly loomed.

'Any questions?' Niven asks. We shake our heads. 'Okay. Let's go. Take care on this path.'

As we near the kissing-gate at the edge of the moor the mist begins to thin and shred. We walk out to an autumn afternoon that is in full sunlight and my eyes begin to water.

The journalists, photographers and TV news crews are gathered at the edge of the gravelly car park, checked in place by four PCSOs who stand in a broken line.

The uniforms move aside after a motion of Niven's hand. DI Bingham indicates where we should wait with him. Niven and Sonia Lister stand in front of us. Digital cameras click and buzz. The TV camera operators look at their viewfinders. Microphones and voice-recorders are held at arm's length. My eyes are momentarily drawn beyond the crowd to lights that are twinkling, changing colours, on a Christmas tree at the entrance to the pub.

Niven moves a pace forward, pauses, seems to take his measure of the ranks of reporters. He has everyone's attention.

'Good afternoon. Thank you for coming. I'm DCI Frank Niven, the Senior Investigating Officer. I'm going to make a brief statement and then I'll invite my colleague, DC Sonia Lister, to speak on behalf of Kath Davy, the sister of Ben Davy. I'll take a few questions after.' He steals a moment to consult a sheet of notes.

'Ben Davy disappeared on the eighteenth of August 1976 when he was eleven years old. He was last seen by his three friends, getting into a van with a man and a woman who have never been identified. A few months ago, Ben's remains were found buried on Burbage Moor. I'm heading the investigation into the abduction and murder of Ben Davy.'

One word hits me heavily, like a blow to the head. *Murder.* I close my eyes and it repeats in my mind while Niven continues to speak. *Murder. Murder. Murder.* It's the word I've avoided saying for years. Ben had been *missing*, that's how I've always thought of him, because it gave me, all of us, hope that one day he might be found alive. But, no. He's dead. He was murdered. We know now, and we've stood at the place where he'd been buried and had lain for almost half a century. How is it possible? How can it be so long ago since that summer?

Sonia Lister begins to read a typewritten statement. Her voice is strong, controlled. She says Ben's family had desperately hoped for him to be found alive, that his parents had gone to their graves still hoping and praying for him, and lastly she asks that Kath's right to privacy be respected.

Ross is holding one of Kath's hands. She has reddened eyes, her head resting against his shoulder, the corners of her mouth are twitching.

Niven invites questions. The reporters shout, fighting to be heard. Niven points. 'The lady at the front, your question? And give your name.'

Please let it be over.

'Hello. Lorna Dudgen. *Sheffield Star*. Can I ask how Ben's friends are feeling today? Would they like to say something about him?'

Dan and Ross immediately look at me. Their faces carry the same message. Over to you mate, step up, take one for the team.

Lorna Dudgen waits. She seems enthusiastic, a little nervous too, with her arm rigidly stretched forward holding a voice recorder, a barely noticeable tremor in her hand. I wonder if this is the biggest assignment she's been given by her editor so far. I know how it feels, getting your first chance of a lead story, being desperate to get it right, dreading careless fuck-ups.

It's too late, all of this, isn't it? How old would they be? I'm fifty-seven for God's sake. They'd be, what, in their eighties? Are they even alive? What's the point? Are the police hoping someone will tip them off after all this time? Or maybe there'll be a deathbed confession from him, or her, after seeing us on the news? A final desperate plea bargain with the Almighty before the end comes. I don't know... I can't... let go of it... knowing I should have... could have stopped him... but I'd hated him right then... and... it feels like... like we're just hopelessly chasing the dead...

I clear my throat, look directly at Lorna Dudgen. The skin around her eyes is still fresh, without shadows, as yet unlined by the job.

'I'm Mike Lorton. When Ben disappeared we were young lads. We've never stopped thinking about him. He was fun to be with, a lovely kid, and I'm sure we all hero-worshipped him more than a bit. He was the undisputed leader of our tight, happy little gang. The three of us have stuck together all these years, but there should have been four of us growing older together.'

And I almost go to pieces now because, for a few shattering moments, I think of all the parties, weddings, New Year piss-ups and weekend trips when Ben should have been there. He isn't getting increasingly grumpy and slightly forgetful with us, nurturing his pension, sarcastically counting down the years to getting his bus pass, having doubts about how much to put aside for a funeral, complaining about his grandkids' addictions to their mobile phones, or joining in our never-ending debates about Brexit. We're greying, or balding, with muscles turning slack and soft, but he's remained a boy who I think of with memories that seem to lose a little more clarity and colour every day.

I cough to stop the wobble in my throat, glance at the ground, and carry on.

'We're all… very sad, and devastated, to know his life was taken in a terrible, awful way. So his sister Kath, and their late parents, can have justice for Ben I'd ask anyone with information that might help the police in their enquiries to come forward. Please, if you have suspicions about someone, contact the police, whatever loyalties you might have.'

More questions fly at me, but I've turned away. Niven gives me a curt nod, mouths, 'Well done.' Kath hugs me. Dan, Ross and Sonia Lister have tears in their eyes. Bingham is implacable, hands together behind him, feet rooted to the spot where he stands. I don't care for him much.

Niven takes a few more questions before raising his hands. 'We're done. That'll be all. Thanks for coming everybody.'

I hold Kath as she presses her face against my chest, realise she's wearing her mum's favourite perfume again, and when she manages to whisper 'Thank you for speaking Mike,' I'm completely broken.

TABLE 4
ABBY WALKER

The breakup was acutely undramatic. I knew it had to be coming – the decline of the relationship had been both steady and obvious – but I hadn't wanted to be the one to call it, for what I'd thought at the time was pity, but recognised later as simple curiosity. How long would Lee last before giving in?

There were several false starts before he did it. One was in a beach-side cafe in Saltburn, when the idle conversation he'd been making petered out, and he looked at me with damp, heavy eyes and I knew he was going to do it, and I knew the second that he did, I was going to run into the sea. Maybe he saw the thought in my face because he gave me a bracing smile and said wasn't it so nice to get out into the fresh air.

Several times I felt it in bed, in the dark, when I knew he was awake too, turning it over in his head, and I'd lie on my back and wait. The pressure would build to a pounding behind my eyes. *Now... Now... Now.*

It came on a random morning after breakfast, an *I don't think this is really the right thing anymore.* I'd had responses ready for every possible thing he could have said, in every shade of emotion – indignant, furious, heartbroken, cruel – but in truth, he caught me off guard. I was standing over the bin, fishing out the few soggy cornflakes from the milk in the bowl. I paused for a couple of seconds. Then spotted another one.

'Lola.'

You had to catch every last one or they'd choke the dishwasher. I was always having to make it sick.

'Did you hear me?'

He sounded guilty.

'Yeah,' I said.

'Okay.'

I swirled the milk around, checking there was nothing hiding beneath, and poured it into the dishwasher. I felt him watch me as I kneed the door shut, and when I looked at him, none of the things I planned to say seemed to fit. I hadn't quite covered every eventuality.

'Yeah, okay,' I said.

* * *

I was quite numb until a couple of days after we both moved out, neither of us being able to cover the rent on our own – me on a barista salary and Lee still with a year of his apprenticeship to go. I hadn't told anyone about the breakup. My friends were Lee's friends first. I hadn't told anyone at work either, not wanting to waste the moment when I wasn't feeling it.

It was a Wednesday I announced it. Rota'd for the opening shift, I didn't get out of bed until ten a.m. I had been awake early, flicking between Instagram and TikTok until a message from Max interrupted.

Table 4

Hi you were supposed to be in at 8 this morning, are you not coming?

I let some time pass. Resumed the true crime YouTube Shorts series. Eleven Shorts later, when the body had been reassembled, I messaged him back.

Hi Max I'm really sorry but Lee and I broke up this morning. Honestly I'm not in a good place but I'm leaving the house now if you can cover for me a bit longer. I really appreciate it, sorry to put you in this position x

I waited in bed another five minutes for his reply.

Call in sick if you want. Don't think Sandy will mind.

No I need to get out of this house ASAP x

Ok.

He went offline. I waited for him to come back on. He didn't.

* * *

Customary commiserations were scattered amongst people at work, and then, rather quickly, order restored. I sensed an irritated vibe from Max after my third *'five mins'* and supposed my moment was over. Lee came into the coffee shop twice in the next couple of weeks, once to drop off a charger he'd accidentally packed away, and once more without reason, which I assumed to mean he missed me. That second time, I saw him coming and turned to Max.

'I don't think I can keep doing this,' I told him.

Max was cleaning out the coffee machine and glanced at Lee, who stood at the counter with his hands in his pockets. I stared down at the floor.

'What can I get you, mate?' Max asked him.

'Green tea, please.'

Max filled a to-go cup with boiling water and dropped the bag inside. He handed it over.

'Maybe it'd be better if you go somewhere else for now, you know,' Max said, not unpleasantly.

There was a pause in which Lee didn't try to catch my eye, though I was now trying hard to catch his.

'Yeah, okay,' he said, and left.

Some of that familiar rage boiled through me and evaporated. I touched Max's arm as he reached past me for the milk stirrers.

'Thank you,' I said.

'It's fine. Can you pass me those?'

I passed them. He took them over to Table 8.

I thought he might have asked me if I was okay, even just so I could say that I was. I could have smiled after, which he would have taken as both brave and desperately sad, and from then on, he might give more than one-word answers to my questions, might actually start to ask some of his own.

He returned to his station and set to making a smoothie.

* * *

There's nothing striking about The Man when he comes in. He's smartly dressed, a black jacket and white shirt, no tie. A MacBook Pro in a leather briefcase-style bag that he brings out onto the table, plugging it into the socket in the wall at his back. I've seen him a couple of times, always in that spot, his screen facing away. We get a few of his kind. More so since the

Table 4

new offices opened up. Most of their screens are spreadsheets and Teams. The only interesting one was last week, when the guy opened Chrome and had to scramble to clear several tabs of racing bets before bringing up a doc. From his stammered apologies, I assumed he was sharing his screen. I turned on the little TV above the counter – no sound – and put on Cheltenham. He chatted in his headphones, nodded to no one, his eyes wandering up to the TV. I watched them glaze over, felt mine glaze too.

The Man is not so interesting at first. He orders an espresso and a glass of iced water. He's either southern or private school. I don't need to wait for the 'o' in 'espresso' to tell. He has a nice, if slightly condescending smile, a pretty face, and I'm not interested.

'I'll bring it over,' I tell him.

A couple of girls come in asking for more smoothies and I do those first. And then a matcha latte. I glance over at The Man and see he's focused on a phone call through his headphones. I tune in as I'm frothing milk.

'...absolutely, darling. No problem, I'll get them on my way in... No, I'm in the office all day today. Back-to-back meetings, this will probably be my only window to talk.'

I finish making another drink before taking over his espresso and water. He sees me coming.

'Sorry – sorry, darling, tell me when I'm home. My manager's just shouted me in, I've got to go. Yes, I'll pick those up. Okay, love you, love you.'

He takes off his headphones. I put down his drinks.

'Thank you,' he says. He doesn't look at me.

Dismissed, I go back to the counter.

It's a slow day, and I keep looking over at The Man. His headphones stay zipped into their case by his laptop, which he seems to tap at every few minutes. He doesn't speak. At one p.m., he orders a mozzarella and pesto panini and an Americano with cold milk. At 4:45 he packs up his things and leaves.

* * *

His girlfriend is called Amanda. I say girlfriend because he doesn't have a wedding ring, though they have a house together and seem pretty settled, in my opinion. He's coming in more often. He always tells Amanda he's busy but I'm not exactly sure what it is he does. He clicks the trackpad periodically, doesn't seem to type much. I wish I could get a glimpse of his screen.

Last night I dreamt of him and Amanda. It's not as odd as it sounds: I'm dreaming more now that I'm sleeping on my own, about all kinds of things. Nothing much happened in the dream. They had me over for dinner and their house was one of those old money New England-type houses you see in American films, with ornate archways and big dining rooms. Amanda was playing piano.

'Debussy,' I said.

'Well done,' The Man said, sat opposite me at the table.

His white shirt was unbuttoned by two. He exchanged a smile with Amanda, one that said weren't they so lucky to have a friend that understood the world and them so well.

The Man took my hand and I smiled at the two of them, my dream-face open and soft.

* * *

Table 4

It was hard to suppress a lurch in my belly when he came in this morning. When I handed him his espresso, our fingers touched beneath the saucer and I remembered how it felt to hold his hand. But the memory of that feeling exists only for me, and he took the cup and saucer from me with perfect indifference.

I clean nearby tables and try to ignore the residual sting. I'm just about to head back to the counter when his phone rings, the headphones going back on his head. I dust the leaves on the artificial succulent on Table 5.

'Hey, darling.'

The *darling* hurts, briefly. Amanda's blonde, I've decided – at least, she was in the dream. She's a schoolteacher. Primary school, in an affluent little village up in Northumberland. There's a piano in the classroom and the kids sing with her around it before home-time, and they draw her pictures that she puts up on her fridge at home.

'Yeah, just getting a coffee... No, not too busy, really... Will do. Listen, my gate's up in ten minutes so I'd better go. I'll give you a call when I land, okay?'

My hand stills over the leaves of the plant.

'Should only be a couple of hours... I will. Love you.'

He winds down the call, takes off his headphones, and zips them into the suitcase at his feet. I hadn't noticed the suitcase before.

He takes a long sip of his coffee and opens something up on his laptop. I watch him. The airport is a good twenty-minute drive from here, thirty more realistically. His legs are stretched long, ankles crossed under the table.

'Lola,' Max calls sharply.

I return to the counter, keeping an eye on The Man as I clear the queue. Thirty minutes pass, an hour, the lunchtime rush. He doesn't move. Between customers, I scroll through Newcastle departures on my phone, trying to find one that would fit the timeline. There are too many. A 'couple' of hours is too vague – it should mean two, but sometimes means three, sometimes one and a half. The heat of the panini oven makes my hair stick to my forehead.

At two p.m., The Man takes his headphones from his suitcase. I go to clean the table next to him.

'Hi darling, just landed. Going to be pretty swamped for the next few days and the reception over here isn't great so I'll just call when I can. Don't worry, okay? I'm going to miss you. I love you.'

He can hear my heart, I know it. There's a familiar pressure rising in my face.

He doesn't take the headphones off. He's waiting for something, staring down at his phone. A phone that is smaller in his hand, the case blue instead of black.

'Hey, sweetheart… I know, I know – listen I've just picked my bags up so I'm headed to yours now… My leave got approved, too, so it's just you and me all week… I've got to go, my Uber's pulling up, I'll see you soon… I love you more. Wait, Chrissy—'

He smiles, his voice goes to butter, and everything in me goes still.

'—I've really missed you.'

* * *

He's not back the next day or the one after. Max is getting frustrated with me and I can't blame him. I'm distracted. I don't

Table 4

like having my back to the door. I rush through drinks and slap paninis haphazardly onto plates, just to get a clear view again.

If he comes back, I want him to speak to me, not Max, for me to have his attention, no matter how fleeting. It's a transaction I have some control of. I can make him wait. I can give him a smile and request, implicitly, one back from him. I can make small talk that he is bound by politeness to parry. It's new territory for me – Lee had always been so underwhelmingly available with his attentions.

I'm dreaming about other things too, of course, lots of things, but I keep dreaming of The Man and Amanda, and now this new player – Chrissy. Chrissy has wavy chocolate hair with caramel highlights, like a Rolo mousse – about the only thing I can stomach at the moment – and she is feistier than Amanda. She gives her opinions straight so you know you can trust her. She is a runner, with a runner's body, and drinks protein shakes from her reusable bottle, which she always cleans out the moment she is finished with it.

The four of us are in the New England-style dining room, Amanda playing piano, Chrissy drinking wine. The two of them and The Man are engaged in an intense but amiable discussion. I am content to listen at first, then think of a perfect anecdote to throw in next. I wait patiently for a gap in the conversation that doesn't come.

The next night, we're in the same room. Amanda mustn't be paying attention because she's catching the wrong keys with the edges of her fingers. Chrissy's glass is bigger than last night, one of those goldfish-bowl gin glasses filled with red wine. The discussion has accelerated to a frenetic pace. I can't quite follow the thread. Someone tells an inside joke that causes the three of them to collapse into laughter. Amanda hits a series of discordant notes, face flushed and filled with tears. I try to laugh with them but my voice is too low and forced, and when I wake up, I lie very still in the empty bed and let the weight of each part of my body sink into the mattress.

* * *

After exactly a week, The Man is back. I can't bring myself to smile at him. I've forgotten how to make small talk; I'm nervous. He doesn't wait for me to say anything before ordering an Americano and a pain au chocolat. This is a new addition. Maybe he and Chrissy haven't been eating. Does he look thinner? Or have they been indulging, gotten into a routine of a mid-morning pastry?

He wheels his suitcase over to his table and I follow behind with his order.

'Been somewhere nice?' I ask.

But I've said it too quietly and he has to ask me to repeat myself.

'I just asked if you'd been somewhere nice.'

'Oh. No, just work.'

I retreat behind the counter. I try not to look over to him anymore. He's a cheater. There is nothing interesting in it. I don't know these people, no matter what my dreams would have me believe. Their words and their smiles and their hands – the ones that know me – aren't real. I'm sure that The Man, if faced with another white, dark-haired woman in her late twenties behind the counter tomorrow, wouldn't be able to tell the difference.

The thought makes me angry. I knew it would.

Table 4

Max brushes past me to grab a cloth and accidentally touches the small of my back. He quickly moves away, muttering an apology.

'It's okay,' I say.

He cleans the coffee machine down, his back to me. Maybe he's blushing. I want to apologise to him, for being so shitty to work with. It hasn't been fair on him. And if I apologise, I can explain – because I owe him an explanation – that it's been hard since the breakup, that being alone has taken its toll, but he doesn't need to worry because I'm going to try my very best not to let all of my baggage affect him.

I play out the conversation in my head and find that I mean it. I'm finished with The Man. He's not even that attractive.

To prove it to myself, I offer to take the drinks Max has prepared to Table 3, the one next to The Man. Max lets me. I walk over with my head up, eyes resolutely ahead. It's easy really. He's in my periphery, of course, headphones on his head, but he's irrelevant now.

I reach Table 3, two girls in their early twenties, and give them their drinks. My small talk not only returns, it flows, and soon the three of us are laughing. They're Newcastle students. Their laughter seems genuine. They find me funny. Perhaps they need an older sister figure, someone to guide them through these anarchic years. Lord knows I could give them some stories.

Buoyed by an abrupt euphoria, I'm about to ask whether they would like to hang out sometime, when I hear his voice, and everything falls away.

'...could do, the flight's been cancelled... I've tried to use it too many times, it's frozen. Would you be able to put some more money on the other card for me?'

The girls are looking at me warily. I can't move. Neither of them reach for their drinks.

'Three hundred should do... Thanks so much, Amanda, really... I'll be home tonight, hell or high water... Okay, darling, I love you.'

One of the girls asks if I'm okay. I manage a stiff nod and go through to the kitchen. I lean over the sink, splash some water on my face. I wipe at the mascara lines down my cheeks.

I know who he is, now. A liar, a cheater, a scammer, a criminal – maybe more. And I know that I'm not done with him yet, because I cannot allow him to continue.

Some of that euphoria fizzes back to life. I need to warn Amanda and Chrissy. It's the decent thing to do.

* * *

In the name of decency, I follow him home to Amanda's. After closing, he gets the Metro from Central Station to Ilford Road, and so do I. From there, we walk until the terraces break up into the wide semi-detached homes and three-storey townhouses of Gosforth. I stand on the corner of the street and watch him knock on the blue front door of a townhouse.

We wait for her to answer.

Sweat drips between my shoulder blades and I realise I'm still wearing my apron.

The door opens and a blonde head appears – *she's blonde!* – but before I can get a look at her face, she wraps her arms around his neck and buries herself there. The Man sets his suitcase, with its two phones inside, into the hall by her bare feet, and walks the two of them inside.

Table 4

He pushes the door closed with his hip.

I stand there a bit longer. I feel odd. A bit dizzy. I write down her address in my notes app and head home.

* * *

The odd feeling persists all night. I shower and run my hands over my neck, down both sides of my collarbones, over my shoulders. It doesn't quite feel real, that she was there in the flesh, just yards from me. Like seeing a celebrity in the wild. That mixture of excitement and familiarity, and the crushing realisation that they have no idea who you are.

I try to hold onto the feelings, feel them deepen and unfurl, revealing at its centre, what I am still, after all this time, surprised to find.

Envy.

* * *

'Contactless is down,' I say. 'You need your card.'

The Man puts his phone in his pocket, the pleasant patronisation his face usually holds hardening. This inconvenience to him is an unintended side effect of my plan, but one I enjoy. Really, I want to see inside his wallet.

He pops open the leather wallet and I lean closer. There are two cards. A credit and a debit. That's all. I had expected the pockets to be filled with cards in different women's names. But of course, he can't be that obvious. Stupid.

He slots his debit card into the reader. I'm just quick enough to catch his name.

Alexander Pinewood.

It doesn't suit him.

'I'll bring it over,' I say, but he's already walking over to Table 4, without a thank-you.

* * *

Who's to say he isn't just a thief and a liar? There are plenty for whom stealing and lying are just the shallows of their misdeeds. For many, they are the gateway to more. It's all about power, with men like him. And I see now that our relationship is built on an imbalance of it, too. I have to be here, and he does not. I have to be polite to him, where he needs only to not abuse me to stay. He knows what he's doing. There are plenty other coffee shops.

I'm beginning to get worried for Amanda and Chrissy, and any other woman involved with him. Extremely worried. I consider going to the police but I'm not sure there's enough to go on, just yet – and is there ever?

It's lonely, being the only one to know what's really happening, and a responsibility, too. If something were to happen to Amanda and Chrissy, it would be my fault.

It's my job, now, to keep the three of us safe.

* * *

I find Chrissy on Twitter. I'm searching for *Alexander Pinewood* when a preview of a Tweet appears on Google.

Me and @alexpinewood having the best time in…

I click on it.

Table 4

This tweet has been deleted.

Alexander's account no longer exists. But the original poster does. Chrissy Lovell @crisslove1991. She's a something in finance. Chrissy Lovell.

Amanda's surname I find through old-fashioned means: I take in a parcel for her. Royal Mail, about 10:20. It only takes four attempts.

Amanda Johnston.

I write it down and throw the parcel over her garden fence.

Amanda loves Twitter, Chrissy loves Instagram, neither seem to love privacy settings. Both lost their parents in the last three years. Both have well-paying jobs. Chrissy is a marketing somebody and fashion influencer with over 200k followers, complete with sponsorships and brand collaborations. Amanda has celebrated a steady stream of promotions. Both love to travel, backpacking around countries I've never heard of, pictured standing in front of statues and buildings that are as familiar to me as Grey's Monument, but that I cannot name.

They are successful, undoubtedly. But there are flaws there, too. Some of Chrissy's photos are a little too posed. Bordering on self-absorbed. Some of Amanda's Tweets are a little too saccharine, self-pitying. After a couple of hours of scrolling, they start to annoy me.

I go for a walk along the Quayside. The water's up, the wind razoring the surface against the current. I can see what he sees in them, despite how annoying they are. Amanda is kind. Chrissy is pretty. I am neither. I have both parents and no money. I've never been, will never be, anywhere but here.

* * *

I call in sick and spend the day scrolling in bed. A grey March evening bleeds under the curtains. At seven, I get up mechanically, pulling on yesterday's clothes, and sit on the edge of my bed. I try to find the excitement. It'll be there. I've lived in my body for almost thirty years now, I know what makes it feel.

The train I follow The Man onto is busy. I face three guys, each on their phones, studiously avoiding each other's faces, each other's knees, squeezed close together in the narrow blue seats. I stare at them. I wonder if they would remember me in a lineup.

We get off at Tynemouth and I have to be careful – he keeps looking behind himself. He keeps checking his phone. I hang back, watch him knock on the door of a detached house with a front yard filled with wildflowers. Chrissy appears long enough to pull him in for a kiss and close the door behind them.

I wait on the corner. Wait until it starts to rain, the clouds bringing in the dusk. Hands in my pockets, I walk slowly past the house. The Man is in the window, searching for something on a bookshelf. He finds what he is looking for and closes the curtains.

I stop on the kerb.

I've forgotten what I came here to do.

* * *

I dream of the four of us around the table again. We've eaten a Sunday dinner. It's getting late but no one turns on a light; the streetlamp outside the window casts a dirty yellow sheen over

Table 4

half of the table. The shadow of the chicken carcass stretches across the other half. No one goes to clean it away. No one says anything. I try to remember the perfect thing I was going to say in the last dream and can't.

* * *

I take the week sick from work, wake on the eighth day refreshed. I clean my flat. I have a long conversation with a nice girl from my phone provider, and am ready again. I can't lose focus. Even annoying women don't deserve to be murdered, and that's what I feel is coming. The game is too elaborate for anything else.

Yes – I can say with almost absolute certainty that either Chrissy or Amanda is about to be killed.

But even almost absolute certainty needs evidence.

It's just a cheap thing from Amazon but it does the job, is small enough to hide inside Table 4's fake plant, sensitive enough to pick up The Man's voice on his calls. I slip the device into my pocket at the end of the shift and plug it into my laptop, which only just manages to open the audio file. Then I put on my headphones and type.

* * *

In two weeks, I have everything I need, printed in a nineteen-page folder.

Today The Man has the Amanda phone on the table, which means he's going home to her. Which means I am going to Chrissy. I remember what I was going to do.

Just before I know he will leave, I make him an Americano on the house. He looks up at me in surprise.

'Thanks,' he says.

'No problem at all.'

I smile wide. I want him to remember my face.

* * *

I wait on the corner of Chrissy's street until it gets dark, just in case I've miscalculated and The Man is about to appear in the yard. But no one approaches the house, and on my several sweeps up the street, there is only Chrissy in the window.

It's after nine. Chrissy has drawn the blind in the bedroom, turned on a lamp.

I go up the three steps to her front door, the folder in my hand. She has a video doorbell. I stare into its glowing blue ring.

Will she confront him? Almost surely. And what will he do in return? If she calls him now, will he come? Will he turn up at the door, soaked through by rain, and with her final ounce of pity, will she invite him in to talk, and will that be her mistake?

Will he look back on the video doorbell and find me, the informant? And what then?

I could linger nearby. I could convince him I can be trusted.

I could help dispose of the body.

It's bin day tomorrow, and there are lots of bins out the back of the coffee shop. I have my key for the back door. The Man and I could sit in the dark of Table 4 afterwards,

Table 4

gathering ourselves until morning. We would have to stick to our usual routines so as not to incur any suspicion, and so he would need to come in a few hours later, in the daylight, and ask for his Americano with hot milk and sit at his table and I would bring it to him as always, except this time there would be something new between us. No eye contact, of course. Too risky. But in the act of not looking, there would be an intimacy. We would need to find somewhere private to talk it over. My place, or his.

I blink and the blue ring of the doorbell is imprinted on the back of my eyelids.

Poor Chrissy.

She has such nice curtains in her living room, a deep maroon. I want to see them from the inside.

I lift my finger to the doorbell. It will only take the barest amount of pressure. A soft click and a chime from the other side.

I look up at her bedroom window. The soft yellow hue of her bedside lamp has gone dark. Her cheek is on her pillow, her hand curled beneath her chin. She smells of fabric softener and hand cream.

I press the doorbell and run.

* * *

That night I'm back in the New England house but I am no longer at the table. I'm in the kitchen, at the sink, looking out of a window into the yard.

I pick a plate out of the sink, streaked with gravy and bubbles, and wash it.

In the window, the door opens behind me and Chrissy walks in carrying three empty wine glasses. She stands by me at the sink. We look at each other's reflections.

'I'm sorry,' I say.

She tuts sadly. 'Lola.'

She pushes the glasses under the water and we wash one each, sharing the sponge, and then the tea towel. Amanda and The Man laugh next door. Amanda is playing a jazz piece on the piano, and Chrissy is smiling softly, and tiredly, and proudly, as if she is seeing it too – everything she has always wanted. She kisses the side of my head and I close my eyes.

'Come on back to the table, sweetheart. Leave all this now.'

* * *

I wake up.

I get out of bed before my alarm, brush my hair and moisturise my face and apply light make-up. I eat cereal at the fold-away table and clean my teeth and lock my front door.

At work, I change into my apron, put my bag in my locker, and open up.

We're busy.

'Are you alright?' Max asks, after a productive but silent hour.

'Yeah.'

His next question is lost in the roar of the boiling tap. He doesn't repeat it and I don't ask him to. I am ever-so-slightly out of focus. As drinks pass through my hands, I watch them start to slow, my arms growing heavy. Max comes from behind and takes a cappuccino cup from me. It has overflowed, the

Table 4

tray beneath the machine full. My finger and thumb are pink. I look at Max and find concern.

I turn away from him, go up to the counter where the next customer waits.

It is The Man.

I stare at him.

'Americano, thanks.'

I'm breathing fast and deep through my nose, like I'm about to be sick.

'No bother mate, I'll bring it over,' Max says, when I've waited too long.

As The Man goes to his table, Max touches my elbow.

'Are you sure you're alright?'

I'm already heading to the break room, unwrapping my apron. I've tied it too tight. I sit on the edge of the chair and close my eyes, but it doesn't bring the comfort I want it to. There's noise from the coffee shop and from the piano in the dining room and I'm in neither. I'm inside the wall between them.

I suck in a wet breath and open my eyes. My chest hurts. I grab my bag from the locker and take out two paracetamol. I swallow them with a cupped hand of tap water. I put the packet back in my bag.

I pause.

Then I grab the folder from it.

I walk back through the kitchen, out from behind the counter, over to Table 4. I sit down. The Man looks up from his laptop, startled. I hand him the folder.

His face is impassive as he reads. This close, I can see the stubble on his cheeks. I wonder, idly, what it would feel like on the back of my hand.

He finishes the last page and closes the folder.

'What do you want?' he says.

His phone is unlocked by his elbow on the table. I reach out to it slowly. Touch it. He lets me. I hold his gaze as I slide it towards me. I open his contacts. Type my number. Type *Lola*.

I lock it and slide it back to him.

He rests his fingers over the black screen, and looks at me. There's a hazel ring around his pupil, though the rest of his iris is blue, the whites perfectly white. They are narrowed slightly, working.

Then they find what they are looking for, and I watch the shift happen. A smoothening. A recognition.

I smile, and he does too.

'Hi, Lola,' he says.

And his voice saying my name sounds exactly as I thought it would.

SKELETONS
BETH BARKER

Three of us from the same street work on the pier, suspended above the green of the Irish Sea. At the start of the season, we lie facedown and flat to watch it, eyes pressed to the slots between creaking planks. Sometimes it glitters metallic, reflecting blades of light, but that day it sloshed and spat, and it was like our stomachs moved with it. We staggered around on our hands and knees, laughing in a seasick spin, then steadied ourselves before looking down again. Girls staring adulthood in the face, its hungry mouth salivating.

* * *

Briony operates the carousel, Emma the waltzer. I cover the shooting star. We are like the sirens we'd learnt about in school, luring in tourists drunk on heat and sugar and lager, distance too – from whatever town or city they come from. Once we secure their belts, we press a button and watch the machines whir into motion. All day, they twirl and clunk, older than we are, and probably our parents too. We are supposed to shout excitedly, pump up the fun with our fists, ensure that everyone has a good time. Instead, we are distracted by the tick of the clock, watching on from our operating booths. Desperate for their pleasure to end so ours can begin. Before each shift, Briony slops baby oil onto our legs and we stretch them out from our plastic kiosks, six pale stems reaching from the shade and into the sun.

* * *

Our boss is called Gareth. His head is bald and gleaming, like the smooth surface of a boiled egg. He is the height of us girls but the width of a door, round body always clad in a stained vest and fraying swim shorts. He has a collection of floral shirts in his office too, like the ones for sale by the beach in Benidorm. If he isn't wearing one to cover his arse and bends over to wrench at a broken ride, we make eyes at each other, laughing aloud to make sure he hears us. Even when we are taking the piss out of him, he loves to be the star of the show. All eyes on him. When we arrive at the fair in the mornings, faces still puffy from not enough sleep, he greets us extravagantly, all bows and raised eyebrows as if mimicking a circus ringmaster. Once we are herded into his office, an out-of-use sweet stall with a laptop and a plug-in fan, he always insists on a group hug. *Roll up, roll up.* Pressing us into his soft body, damp with sweat and spongy, as if it might absorb us whole. *Gary's angels*, he says, voice hot and breathy.

* * *

At the beginning of the summer, most nights after work were the same. Together, we'd flee the promenade, candy-floss sky merging blue into pink behind us, running wild like alley cats, darting between bodies queuing for mustard-smeared hot dogs and greasy donuts crusted with sugar. As we left the drumming fairground music behind, new sounds replaced it: wailing from the flashing karaoke bar; rowdy blokes in football shirts spilling into the street for a smoke; a drag queen, playing Cher on repeat through a portable CD player, heaving a cart full of light-up hats emblazoned with the Blackpool Tower. Soon though, we were back on our territory with our chests puffed out. Strutting through streets we knew better than the marks on our own skin.

* * *

On our dead-end road, every house looks the same as the next. You can walk from one end to the other in thirty seconds flat. Emma and Briony are neighbours, separated by the thin walls of their red-brick terraces. My bedroom is on the top floor opposite. The tarmac between us is so narrow that I am almost close enough to watch them sleep, and if I lean out my window and look left past the buildings that jut out like crooked teeth, I can trace the line of the sea scrawled across the horizon, and the blank space beyond it.

* * *

Tonight, we come back to find some kids have dragged a trampoline onto the far end of the street, abandoned with its netting torn and springs rusted. Briony skips into her house and returns with three cans of cider as we hoist ourselves onto the plastic. Emma unzips her bag, patent and heart-shaped, pulling out a tin of tobacco, some papers and a strip of filters. We are surprised, glancing at each other, watching as she sits cross-legged and rolls a trio of perfect cigarettes. Effortlessly shaping, licking and tapping them against the tin to get them just right. A conspiratorial smile when she is done. I wonder when she'd mastered the skill, since we'd only ever shared the slender Richmonds she'd robbed from her mum's handbag. I wonder, and could see Briony wondering too, when we'd started keeping secrets.

* * *

On the trampoline, we stare up at the sky that changes colour like a mood ring. Even though the sun has already sunk behind the rooftops and into the sea, we can hear our sticky legs peel away each time we reposition ourselves. I try to plait Briony's hair like Emma's – hers is dark, threaded rope-like down her back, finished with her signature black ribbon – but Briony's is too short and wiry, the blonde curls wild in the humidity. We talk about school, our last days, the people we'll miss and the people we never want to see again. Briony says Max Peters, a bull-necked boy who she has fancied since we were seven years old, is officially dead to her. Even if he did finally push his briny tongue into her mouth at a party last weekend. And even if she did kind of enjoy it. Emma says she is right, *totally*. It is time to move on to bigger and better things. We recall the burning ceremony we'd managed to get invited to, where half of our year gathered to set fire to our blazers and ties in a heap on the sand dunes. Watched as the bonfire threw up a plume of smoke that hung in the air, then caught on the expanding lump in the back of my throat. I had scrunched up my sports kit instead and chucked it quickly into the flames, my pristine uniform still tucked away safely in a box under my bed.

* * *

As Emma pushes the end of another rollie into her empty can and Briony starts on my hair, the popping of an engine startles us. It bursts again, then turns into a spluttering growl that grows closer and closer until the black Ford Fiesta screeches into view. We immediately sit up, necks long and ears pricked, anticipating a threat. In silence, we watch as Daryl, Briony's older brother, lurches from the driver's side, followed by more boys than the car's back seats allow for. Briony rolls her eyes and drops back to a slouch, while I flip open my phone, pretending to text but scrolling through my contacts instead. Emma is still watching them, glare unwavering.

* * *

Alright girls, the shortest one jeers as they walk towards us. He is wearing a matching three-stripe tracksuit and a white baseball cap, stark against his sunburnt neck. An unlit cigarette hangs loose from the corner of his mouth, like someone from one of the crackling Westerns my dad watches on TV. I imagine the recognisable twang of the soundtrack building in intensity, reverberating as they close in. Emboldened, another boy with bare, muscular legs makes his way to the front of the group.

Looking fit as ever ladies, he says, dragging out the S in a bid to sound casual. He wears a cap too, tips it in our direction. *Any of you up for some fun tonight?*

Briony releases a snort – a mistake – then covers her face with her hands as if to shield herself from her own embarrassment. Even though Emma remains composed, her eyes locked on them, I can see the blood pulsing red in her cheeks.

Jesus man, that's his sister, the short one interrupts as he shoves his lanky friend from the group, glancing to Daryl for approval.

I didn't mean that one, obviously.

Yeah, yeah mate, whatever you say, he replies, the rest of them cackling behind him.

Daryl doesn't say anything. We are used to him ignoring us, so I am unsure if I am imagining it when he offers a slight nod before they file into Briony's house. Maybe it is because we are adults now. Sharp-clawed animals let loose from the confines of the school gates. Released into *their* world, one we believed to be full of substance and possibility, but so far doesn't feel any different at all.

* * *

A text: one of the lads from the pier is having a party and we are all invited. We pound into Emma's house in unison, through the hall, past the living room where her mum lies unconscious on the sofa in front of the ten o'clock news. Our ritual plays out. Bedroom door slammed shut and the stereo ramped up, *Clubland Classics* disc spinning inside. Standing mirror lying horizontal so each of us can take a space on the floor in front of it. Our hands collide as we rifle through a shoebox full of make-up, hair pins, lotions – all sticky and coated in something that smells sickly sweet. Briony asks Emma to do her face just like hers and she does, eyes lined thick with black and smudged at the edges. She offers to do mine too, but I tell her I am trying something new tonight, lids already dusted electric blue. I tilt my head to show her and she smiles, nods, blows a kiss in my direction. She approves. Within the hour we are ready and roaming again, into the night.

* * *

The morning after. We man our stations with dry mouths and tired eyes. Gareth barks at Briony for leaving the carousel unattended, then again when she swears the splatter of bile fizzing behind her booth doesn't belong to her. As usual, he praises Emma for the dizzied crowds spilling off the waltzer, taking on the over-familiar voice of someone petting a stranger's dog, leaning over her as he does it, one hand on the control panel while the other fingers the ribbon draped down her back. I shout him over instinctively and invent a question I already know the answer to. I hum obediently as he explains the inner workings of the shooting star – high pressure air, metal cylinders, well-greased pistons to keep things *lubricated*. He raises an eyebrow and I avert my eyes as if it will help to stem the flow of blood to my cheeks, look to Emma instead, now occupying the unwanted desires of another man entirely.

* * *

The sun cooks through the clouds as I move back and forth between my booth and the base of the ride, unfastening and fastening again the fabric straps holding each child precariously in place. Their screams are cutting, all part of a performance, designed to make sure their parents are still watching from behind the barriers below. As the ride inhales, then exhales on its first descent, I think of last night's party: crammed out garage heavy with smoke, filled with the shapes of boys I didn't recognise and a few girls too, sat in laps or gathered in packs, plotting their next move. Emma taking my hand and then Briony's, pulling us through the fog, twisting as we go, slick skin shimmering under a disco light slung from the roof and throbbing in technicolour. One vodka lemonade after another until a feeling of weightlessness, like when a roller coaster drops from its peak and everything inside comes undone.

* * *

Rumours of an impending heatwave turn out to be true and I wake in the belly of it, stuck to the sheets of my bed. It is only just dawn, light pressing gently through darkness. I kneel up onto the mattress and push open the window. Outside, I see Daryl. He is leaning against his car under the streetlight, finishing a cigarette, still wearing his leather bomber jacket despite the stale heat. He runs his hands through his limp hair and it looks the same as it did before, and when he sees someone coming he does it again. I stay low and steady myself against the window ledge. First, there is a hug and an awkward pressing of lips, followed by the familiar engine coughing sleep from its throat. Then, Emma: oil-black hair shining, climbing into the car before its surface slips out of view.

* * *

I want to tell Briony what I have seen, but I think better of it. Our unspoken rules state that Emma should be the one to have that conversation. That's how it works in a group of three. I clutch the secret tightly like I do with the gold cross around my neck, except this new talisman doesn't bring me comfort. I feel sick with the knowledge of it, so much so that I text Gareth and tell him I am too ill to work today. I text Emma too, then send the same message to Briony, careful in my phrasing to avoid any questions.

Bad stomach (gross), not working today. C u tomorrow xxx

Briony replies, offering to bunk off too. Nothing from Emma. I hold down the power button until the screen's light fizzles out.

* * *

At home, I laze around downstairs and gulp at a glass of water, yesterday's hangover still lingering. While he waits for the kettle to boil, Dad comes into the back room and asks if I've thought about college yet, perched on the edge of the sofa.

Have you decided what subjects you'll take?

I tell him I am not sure, too much to choose from. And besides, results day is still a while off.

But it's so exciting, isn't it? he says, squeezing my shoulders playfully, hands clammy in the heat. I hide my smile behind a cushion.

My clever daughter, aye? A-levels first, uni next. You'll be able to do anything and go anywhere you like, kid. It's all so exciting. Get out while you still can.

I nod, feigning enthusiasm, the weight of *getting out* and what it means settling on my chest. Saved from further interrogation by the click of the kettle. I am excited, yes, but the thought of leaving – this place, the people in it – pulls my guts into a knot that I can't untangle. Even if it is years away. I take out my phone, switch it back on, think about sending a text: *I don't want summer to end I don't want to grow up I don't want to lose what we have* – then decide against it and bury my face under the cushion again.

* * *

After work, Briony knocks on and Dad sends her upstairs. She dives onto the bed and grabs the book I am reading from my hands, throws it to the floor.

No studying in the holidays, she says, lying on her front and framing a toothy grin with her hands. She's chewing bubblegum, wet and fleshy, lips slapping as she manoeuvres it from one side of her mouth to the other.

How's the tummy?

Better, I lie. I might not actually be ill, but the combination of the oppressive heat and the ache of seeing something

I shouldn't have is enough to make me feel it. She pats my stomach gently, childlike, and suddenly it is like we are in primary school again playing pretend. Emma always the discerning doctor, Briony her loyal nurse, and me, the willing patient. My eyes well and suddenly there is an urge to speak in a bid to stop myself crying.

Emma's been seeing Daryl, I blurt. *I think she is anyway. I saw them together. I haven't asked her about it.*

I wait. There is a look of surprise that I think might turn into anger, an expression reaching a boil, but instead it fades away. She sits up, takes out her gum, presses it onto the coaster on my bedside table. I look at it and then back at her, never not alarmed by her brashness but used to it all the same.

I know. Weird, isn't it? I mean, I don't care. But weird she wouldn't tell us.

Yeah, I reply. *It is weird.* I am unsure of how she already knows. Unsure of why, out of all the things to take well, she has chosen this one.

I can't believe she's been texting one of our old teachers too, she scoffs nervously, looks to me for a reaction. *It's sick,* she adds when I say nothing, my mouth gasping for the right words. *And she wasn't at work today either. Did she text you? She didn't text me.* Briony rolls into an awkward laugh and shuffles towards the end of the bed, as if she is wary of what I might do next.

A teacher? Who? I snap, swallowing hard to contain the acid rising in my throat.

Fuck knows. She unwraps another rectangle of gum, macerates it to pulp. Her eyes flash sharp momentarily before softening again.

Just another one of her many skeletons, I guess.

* * *

The next day, I start work earlier than the others. Gareth has asked me to help with the stocktake – a meaningless activity, since we all know he fiddles the books anyway to cover up however many crates of beer he's stolen from the pier that week. The humidity is almost unbearable, murky clouds reflecting grey in the slopping sea below. Behind the bar, I start counting how many bottles are left in the fridges and write each number on the back of a discarded receipt. My phone vibrates in my back pocket and I hope it is from Emma. I imagine opening a long message that explains everything, all the things I already know and anything else she's been keeping from me. Most of all, I am desperate for her to tell me something that will seal up the void that has cracked open between us. She hasn't replied since my sick day, the last image I have of her unrecognisable, climbing into the car without looking back. I hold a glass bottle against the back of my neck and feel relief in the sour heat of the bar, condensation beading down my spine instead of sweat. The text is from Mum: *I'll be out when ur home, but tea is in fridge xx*

Emma will be here soon, in time for the Saturday night shift. I can already smell the oil bubbling hot in the deep fryers and salty popcorn, kept warm against the metal drum. I'll talk to her when she gets here, I think, rehearsing my lines as I finish the count.

* * *

It took Emma's parents a week to report her missing, then another three for the police to take her disappearance seriously. Daryl was gone for a while too – absent from his plastering job, the seedy pub where he plays pool, the spot on the street outside my window – so it was concluded that they must have run away together. Most girls like us who go missing are categorised in this way, *runaways*, assumed to be feral and out of control, desperate to leave our horrible lives behind. Eventually, when Daryl showed up, claiming to have been on a two-week bender with no Emma in sight, they printed a photo of her on the front page of *The Gazette* with the headline: BLACKPOOL TEEN MISSING FOR OVER A WEEK. And when Daryl was later arrested, more headlines and commentaries followed. Never naming him, but everyone knew. They published photos of Emma's house too, close-ups of the state of the brickwork, explanations on how broken homes produce broken people.

I have been inside since the day the police were called, only getting as far as the bottom of the stairs before collapsing again inconsolably. My parents remind me it is almost time to start college, to start the next chapter, but I am still stuck on the last one, replaying the same events over and over. I lie in bed, thinking about how I'd hammered at the front door the day after she didn't show up to work, eyes streaming. Briony standing sheepishly behind me while Emma's dad, wine-drunk and struggling to hold himself up against the frame, told us to piss off and get a life of our own. *She's not here*, he'd slurred, *she's out doing god knows what, with god knows who.*

Then the interview with the police officer, coffee spilled down her shirt and a hawkish Scottish accent I could barely unpick. I'd sat on the sofa in what felt like a disused staff room, reeling off whatever came to mind in a blur. The friendship we had all shared since we were crawling, the way the three of us could communicate without saying anything at all – as if we were telepathic, or connected somehow, in a way I couldn't explain. The rumbling car, the texts with the teacher I couldn't name, Gareth and his oily fingers, the glances I could translate for so long and now made no sense to me. Shaking my head in an attempt to unearth some known truth, but instead listing off all the ways Emma was at risk and the people who made it so. A man in the corner shop who'd licked his lips in our direction. The goth from the hook-a-duck who'd asked for her number more times than we could count. Growing pitiful and more perplexed then, the officer's voice cutting through the noise: *focus on the facts, lovey, focus on the things you know to be true.*

When Daryl is released without charge, dropped from the police car and ushered into the house, his face gaunt and self-conscious, I am confused. It seemed like the most obvious explanation. Despite this, and even though I've barely spoken to Briony since his arrest, unable to text or talk normally without Emma's name, or his name, leaking out of us and widening the chasm, I am still relieved for our friendship. I look out the window, across the street to their house, glass and woodwork dripping with the word MURDERER, spelled out in spray paint the colour of blood. I wonder how she feels about all of this, but I can't bear to ask. Mum said they might be moving away because of it all, that I should try to say my goodbyes soon. I am starting to think that leaving this place might not be such a bad thing after all.

Each day, I sit on my knees in front of my parents, begging them to call the station again to find out what's happening.

They share a look of worry, as if they know something I don't. They give in to my demands, but every time the answer is the same. *The investigation is ongoing. There are no further updates at this time.* Mum's face slouches into ugly sympathy as soon as the line goes dead. Dad strokes my back as we sit in front of the TV, watching the soaps as if my entire existence has not been jolted from its axis. They're careful to avoid the news channel. I stare blankly and create a mental list of the words used to describe someone who is missing. *Absent* is the easiest to digest – it feels temporary, like having a day off sick or skipping school to go on holiday a week early to avoid the highest prices. Next, there's *vanished / disappeared / misplaced*, all suggesting Emma could be part of some elaborate magic trick and we're just waiting for the grand reveal. I picture her swooping down from a wire, or poking her head out from a box and her feet from another, body neatly sliced in two. Last on the list – *dead* – the word I can't fully form, pushing my tongue into the roof of my mouth to stop it from coming. *No news is good news,* I whisper instead like an incantation, though I am old enough to know this is rarely true.

The last week of August – still no sign of her. The feeling of loss, like a part of myself is missing, turns into rage. It's cell-deep and spreading, thrumming through my veins, behind my eyes, in my ears. The town is angry too, tired of one arrest after another leading nowhere. The newspapers and the gossip that follows fuels the fire, and the fear. People gather on the seafront and march through the streets, insisting on better protection for our girls. Applying their own beliefs and grievances to her disappearance. Men wrapped in England flags claim to know *who* has probably or definitely snatched her, setting fire to bins as they go, while mothers hold candles arm-in-arm, internally thankful that it was someone else's daughter and not their own. They demand action, but all I want is Emma.

I speak to Briony on the phone, the night before she leaves Blackpool for good. At first we say little and when we do speak, we talk over each other by accident and retreat to silence instead.

It wasn't Daryl, I promise you it wasn't Daryl, she says eventually, catching her breath.

I know, I say, though I'm not quite sure if I mean it.

They kept him for ages and he was in bits. I've never seen him like that, seriously. When he came back, he was a different person. We all sat round the living room and he crouched there on the carpet sobbing like a little kid. He said they'd gone for a drive, had a kiss or whatever near the dunes, then she'd asked him to drop her off by the pier on their way back down the prom. He asked why but she didn't tell him, just said it was something she had to do.

As she explains, voice pitchy and desperate, questions begin to queue up in my mouth. How do they know he actually dropped her? Were there any cameras? Where the hell was she going at that time, the pier was surely closed?

The line goes quiet while I think about what to say. I realise she is crying, swallowing loudly to keep her voice from cracking.

I don't know what happened, she says, *I just don't know. But they let him go, didn't they? That's got to mean something?*

I try to accept that, consider the thought for a while. But really, nothing means anything until Emma returns safe and well.

I've got to get off the phone now, but can we keep in touch? When all of this is over, when they find her, I'll come visit and everything will go back to the way it was before. I just know it.

Quiet again, just soft breaths rallying back and forth.

But I don't think— I start to say, before realising the line is dead.

* * *

Desperate for answers, I decide to retrace her steps, starting at the school gates and making my way through every place we've ever been together. When I reach the town centre, I pace the swirling carpets of the arcade. Look around at the crowds craning over slot machines, copper-stained palms pressed hard against the glass, a large billboard advert for the pier behind them, its long neck stretching out into the sea. I remember coming here one summer years ago, just me and Emma. My mum, hairdresser by day and for the rest of the street too, had cut ours the same – two brown bobs swinging as we sprung up the stairs to the ghost train. It's a kid's ride, set above the rest of the arcade. As our carriage trundled through the tunnels, past the neon fangs of a paper sea monster and the red eyes of something blinking in the dark, she reached for my hand and held onto it so tightly my bones ached. And when the lights flashed in a rage as if to mimic a storm, my heart thumping with childish adrenaline, her face twisted up with terror. After, as we shared the first sips of a cold Coke, she looked shaken, deep in thought. Clung to the can and asked, *Why d'you think people like rides that scare them?* I shrugged, unsure of what to say. She seemed upset then, as if she had been hoping for a concrete answer. *Things are scary enough as it is, don't you think?*

When I arrive back on my street after a lot of walking and getting nowhere, the rain starts to come down hard, roiling against the tarmac until the air smells like diesel. It's the kind that brings relief after days of swollen heat and I stand in it for a while, water soaking through my trainers, holding the top of my bag closed to avoid the contents getting wet. It's quiet – everyone has fled the incoming storm and the street is strewn with deserted paddling pools, deckchairs and beer cans. Now the family have gone, driven out by shame, Briony's door has been hammered shut with a plank of wood, *to keep out the squatters*, Dad says, while Emma's looks the same as it always has. A feeling radiates as I position myself in front of it. Maybe it is the venom pooling deep in my stomach, or the curiosity to understand how everything went so wrong. It could be naive faith in the belief that the things we lose are often hiding in plain sight, right where we left them. Whatever it is, one thing is certain: as the sky splits open with thunder, I am grasping the slippery handle, pushing open the door and stepping inside.

The house is empty, and her room is just as it was the last time we were here. A lingering smell of damp, made worse by the dank summer heat. The walls are salmon pink, though mostly covered in posters, magazine cuttings and photos. A timeline of our lives stuck up with Blu-Tack, some newer and others almost sun-bleached to white. It feels strange to be here without her and my hands tremble, partly out of fear that her parents might come back and find me, but because it feels like an intrusion too. I've been here hundreds of times, but never without Emma. Even though everyone says she's probably dead, announced with confidence in the same way they speculate about football scores or reality TV, I still expect her to walk in at any moment.

* * *

The beach is vast and still, hunkered low under an early autumn mist so thick, I can barely make out the shoreline beyond it. I sit on the steps that cascade down to the sand, the exact spot where we've met the night before a new school term for as long as I can remember.

Last year, the three of us had held hands, watching the sun dissolve into a red haze on the horizon. Aware that change was heading towards us full throttle, excited but secretly fearful, not quite knowing what shape it might take.

I imagine what Emma might be doing now, if she has run away. She always talked about going to New York one day, had torn out a photo of Central Park from a travel brochure, its trees scorched fiery orange. *I want to go places*, she'd say. When we asked where, to do what, she'd jump up and shout, *Literally anywhere, anywhere but here*. I think I've always known there'd be a time when she would outgrow us, but I hadn't thought about why she would want to leave until it actually happened. This place has never been good to her, not really. Not in the same way it's been good to me. I wonder if, maybe, she's hiding out in the next town instead, staring out at the same coastline, ready to start anew.

The tide is coming in fast and a cold wind with it. Just as I am about to leave, I glance out at the beach for one last time and notice something moving among the pebbles. I narrow my eyes and move closer, realising what it is. At the sand's edge, I nudge the rocks with my boot, and once released, it jumps up, hovers a little. Drifts from the ground, then catches a breeze and flickers up again. I reach out and try to grab it, but it darts free; twirling, coiling, spiralling above my head. A wave crashes down, filling the air with salt spray as I breathe it in, unable to close my mouth. Then, with one final gust, it dances kite-like into the distance. Out of view, into the unknown: a black satin ribbon, shiny tail whipping in the wind.

ABOUT THE AUTHORS

Inés G. Labarta is a migrant, queer author with a taste for all things dark. She's published six books, including the horror novella *McTavish Manor* (Holland House, 2016). Her latest novel, *The Three Lives of St Ciarán* (Blackwater Press, 2024), blends in magic realism with alternative history. She has a PhD in Creative Writing and lectures at Lancaster University.

Ewan A. Dougall was born and raised in Glasgow, Scotland, which is probably why his stories are usually full of rain. He's always been a fan of the stylised worlds of Raymond Chandler and Philip Kerr, and stories of knights in tarnished armour who lose more often than they win. Ewan is supported by his wife and two cats and can be found on Instagram frequently dressed as a superhero (@ewandougall).

Joey McGarvey is northern-born, yet his DNA is 100% Irish and, indeed, 100% Northwest Donegal. He lives in Cheshire and works for the Royal Literary Fund.

Lauren Archer is a writer of the gothic, strange and surreal. Her work has been published by Fly on the Wall, Writers & Artists and Crow & Cross Keys.

Stan Fenton is the nom-de-plume of a literary fiction writer based in Southport. Stan writes, runs and ruminates up and down the beaches and dunes of the Sefton coast. Stan's stories are gritty and witty, but never cosy.

David Lawrie is a self-taught writer from Hull currently living in Northern Ireland. He is an advocate for spending more time offline and is driven by a ravenous need to write the kind of stories that show up the con job of generative AI (which is, quite frankly, bullshit).

Dan Howarth is the author of the novel *Last Night of Freedom* – a stag party horror thriller, and *Territory* – a snowbound survival novella. He lives on the Wirral with his family and insane dog.

Dawn Nicholson's writing has been published in the Asham Award anthology *Once Upon A Time There Was A Traveller*, *Image* and *Stylist* magazines. Her first novel, *All the Time It Took*, was shortlisted for the Book Edit Writers Prize and longlisted for the Mslexia Novel Award. Extracts from her memoir about caring for her father-in-law, who had dementia, have been serialised in *Caring* magazine. Dawn grew up in Grimsby but now lives in the Yorkshire Dales, where she can often be found walking her Springer Spaniel on the hills around Wensleydale.

Andrew Hudson is a technical writer by day and is technically a writer by night as well. He edits *Mythaxis Magazine* and writes in a variety of genres, now including crime.

Pete Hardy was born, and still lives, in South Yorkshire. He had a long and varied career in financial services. He's enjoyed exploring the moors and mountains of the Peak District and Lake District for more than thirty years.

Abby Walker is a County Durham writer, currently in her final year of an MFA with Manchester Writing School. She was the winner of the 2024 Finchale Award for Short Fiction as part of the Northern Writers Awards, was selected for the 2024/25 cohort of the London Library Emerging Writers Programme, and was the recipient of a Faber Academy scholarship for their Writing A Novel course. Her current work-in-progress is a gothic horror, haunted house novel set in the North-East in the 1920s.

Beth Barker is a writer from Blackpool. She is currently completing her MA in Creative Writing at Manchester Writing School. Her work is interested in all things dark and unsettling.

About Dead Ink

Dead Ink is a publisher of bold new fiction based in Liverpool. We're an Arts Council England National Portfolio Organisation.

If you would like to keep up to date with what we're up to, check out our website and join our mailing list.

www.deadinkbooks.com | @deadinkbooks